# BEFORE I

(A MACKENZIE WHITE MYSTERY—BOOK 4)

## BLAKE PIERCE

## BOOKS BY BLAKE PIERCE

### RILEY PAIGE MYSTERY SERIES
ONCE GONE (Book #1)
ONCE TAKEN (Book #2)
ONCE CRAVED (Book #3)
ONCE LURED (Book #4)
ONCE HUNTED (Book #5)
ONCE PINED (Book #6)
ONCE FORSAKEN (Book #7)

### MACKENZIE WHITE MYSTERY SERIES
BEFORE HE KILLS (Book #1)
BEFORE HE SEES (Book #2)
BEFORE HE COVETS (Book #3)
BEFORE HE TAKES (Book #4)
BEFORE HE NEEDS (Book #5)

### AVERY BLACK MYSTERY SERIES
CAUSE TO KILL (Book #1)
CAUSE TO RUN (Book #2)
CAUSE TO HIDE (Book #3)
CAUSE TO FEAR (Book #4)

### KERI LOCKE MYSTERY SERIES
A TRACE OF DEATH (Book #1)
A TRACE OF MUDER (Book #2)

# PROLOGUE

This would be the last time she did a book signing in some small town no one had ever heard of. She needed to speak to her publicity manager and let him know that just because a town has a bookstore, it is not a major metropolis. Sure, she might seem like a high-maintenance diva by making such a request, but she didn't care.

It was 10:35 at night and Delores Manning was driving down a two-lane road in some long-forgotten neck of the woods in Iowa. She was well aware that she had made a wrong turn about ten miles back because it was shortly after that when her GPS had crapped out. No signal. Of course. It was just the cherry on top of what had been a miserable weekend.

Delores had been on this stretch of road for at least ten minutes. She'd seen no stop signs, no houses, nothing. Just trees and a surprisingly gorgeous night sky overhead. She was seriously thinking about just stopping in the middle of the road and pulling a U-turn.

The more she thought about it, the more that seemed like a good idea.

She was about to hit her brake pedal to come to a stop when a popping sound filled the car. Delores cried out in fear and surprise, but her scream was drowned out by the sudden *thunk* of the car as it seemed to drop several inches and then careened hard to the left.

She managed to jerk the car back into a somewhat straight course but realized that she could not fight against it—there was too much drag. Giving up the fight, she managed to guide the car to the side of the road, parking it a little more than half off of the pavement. She cut her hazard lights on and let out a heavy sigh.

"Shit," she said.

*That sounded like a tire,* she thought to herself. *And if that's the case…hell, I don't even remember if there's a spare in the trunk. That's what I get for taking this deathtrap of a car with me everywhere. You're about to be a bigshot author, girl. Spring some money on planes and rental cars every now and then, huh?*

She popped the trunk release, opened the door, and stepped out into the night. There was a nip to the air, as winter was bearing down on the Midwest, sneaking in behind fall. She pulled her coat tight to her body and then pulled her cell phone out. She was not at all surprised to see the No Service reading; she'd been seeing it continuously for the last twenty minutes or so, ever since her GPS app had stopped working.

She looked at her tires and saw that both the front and the rear on the driver's side were flat. More than that, they were pancaked. She saw something glimmering out of the front tire and dropped to a knee to see what it was.

*Glass,* she thought. *Really? How did glass pop my tires?*

She looked to the back tire and saw several large shards of it sticking through. She glanced back down the road and could see no signs of anything. But that meant nothing because the moon was mostly hidden behind the treetops and it was dark as hell out.

She went to the trunk, already knowing that anything she found would be pointless. Even if there *was* a spare back there, she needed two.

Furious and a bit scared, she slammed the trunk, not even bothering to check. She grabbed her phone and, feeling like an idiot, scrambled up onto the back of the car. She held her phone up, hoping for just a single bar of service.

Nothing.

*Don't freak out,* she thought. *Yes, you're in the middle of nowhere. But* someone *will come by eventually. All roads lead somewhere, right?*

Unable to believe the way this weekend had gone, she got back in her car, where the heater was still doing its work. She angled her rearview mirror so she'd see any headlights approaching from behind and then looked ahead to keep an eye out for any coming straight ahead.

As she ruminated on the failed book signing, the small publicity mix-up, and her most recent trouble of having two blown tires on the side of the road, she saw headlights approaching from ahead. She'd only been waiting for about seven minutes, so she counted herself lucky.

She cracked her door open, providing the overhead light to join the already blinking hazards lights. She stepped out and stayed close to the car, flagging down the approaching truck. She was instantly relieved when she saw that it was slowing down. It veered over into her lane and parked nose to nose with her. The driver switched on his hazards and then stepped out.

"Hey there," said the forty-something man who stepped out of the truck.

"Hey," Delores said. She sized him up, still too pissed at the situation to be cautious of a random stranger who had pulled over so late at night to help her.

"Car trouble?" he asked.

"Tons of it," Delores said, gesturing to her tires. "Two blown tires at once. Can you believe it?"

"Oh, that's terrible," he said. "Have you called Triple A or a garage or anything?"

"No service," she said. She almost added *I'm not exactly from around here* but then decided not to.

"Well, you can use mine," he said. "I usually get at least two bars out here."

He stepped forward, reaching into his pocket for his phone.

Only it was not a phone he pulled out. She was actually very confused at what she was seeing. It made no sense. She couldn't figure out what it was and—

Suddenly, it was coming at her face, very quickly. A split second before she was struck, she saw the shape and shine of what he had slipped over his fingers.

Brass knuckles.

She heard the sound of them striking her forehead, felt a flash of pain, and then a moment later her knees buckled, and she felt herself collapsing onto the hard road. The last thing she was aware of was the man reaching down for her almost caringly, his headlights shining in her eyes, before the world went black.

# CHAPTER ONE

Mackenzie White stood beneath a black umbrella and watched the casket get lowered into the ground as the rain picked up to a steady downpour. The weeping of those in attendance was nearly drowned out by the raindrops on the cemetery grounds and the nearby tombstones.

She watched with a pang of sadness as her old partner spent his last moments among the world of the living.

The casket inched into the grave on the steel runners it had been sitting on during the service while those closest to Bryers stood by. Most of the procession had scattered after the pastor's final words, but those closest to him remained.

Mackenzie stood to the side, two rows over. It occurred to her that although she and Bryers had put their lives in each other's hands on several occasions, she really had not known him all that well. This was proven by the fact that she had no idea who the people that had stayed back to watch him lowered into the ground were. There was a man who looked to be in his thirties and two women, huddled together under the black tarp, having one last moment with him.

As Mackenzie turned away, she noticed an older woman standing another row back, holding her own umbrella. She was dressed in all black and looked quite pretty standing in the rain. Her hair was completely gray, pulled back in a bun, but she looked young somehow. Mackenzie gave her a nod as she headed past her.

"Did you know Jimmy?" the woman asked her all of a sudden.

*Jimmy?*

It took her a while to realize that the woman was talking about Bryers. Mackenzie had only ever heard his first name one or two times. He'd always just been Bryers to her.

*Maybe we weren't as close as I thought.*

"I did," Mackenzie said. "We worked together. How about you?"

"Ex-wife," she said. With a shaky sigh, she added: "He was such a good man."

*Ex-wife? God, I* really *didn't know him.* But in the back of her head, she could recall a conversation during one of their long car rides where he had mentioned having been married in the past.

"Yes, he was," Mackenzie said.

She wanted to tell the woman about the times Bryers had guided her in her career and even saved her life. But she figured

4

there was a reason the woman had distanced herself rather than join the three huddled figures under the tarp.

"Were you close to him?" the ex asked.

*I thought I was,* Mackenzie said, looking back to the graveside with regret. Her answer was simpler, though. "Not very."

She then turned away from the woman with a grieved smile and headed for her car. She thought about Bryers…his dry smile, the way he rarely laughed but when he did it was nearly explosive. She then thought of what work might be like now. Sure, it was selfish, but she couldn't help but wonder how her working environment would be changed now that her partner and the man who had essentially taken her under his wing was dead. Would she get a new partner? Would her position change and have her sitting behind a desk or on some lousy beat with no real purpose?

*God, stop thinking about yourself,* she thought.

The rain continued to pelt down on the umbrella. It was so deafening that Mackenzie almost didn't hear her phone ringing in her coat pocket.

She fumbled it out of her pocket as she unlocked her car door, stowed the umbrella away, and stepped inside out of the rain.

"This is White."

"White, it's McGrath. Are you at the graveside service?"

"Leaving just now," she said.

"I truly am sorry about Bryers. He was a good man. A damned fine agent, too."

"Yeah, he was," Mackenzie said.

But when she peered back through the rain to the graveside, she felt like she hadn't really known Bryers at all.

"I hate to interrupt, but I need you back here. Come by my office, would you?"

She felt her heart skip a beat. It sounded serious.

"What is it?" she asked.

He paused, as if debating whether to tell her, then finally said: "A new case."

***

When she arrived outside of McGrath's office, Mackenzie saw Lee Harrison sitting in the waiting area. She remembered him as the agent who had been assigned as her temporary partner when Bryers had fallen ill. They had gotten to know one another over the last several weeks but had not really had the chance to work together yet. He seemed like an okay agent—maybe a little too cautious for Mackenzie's tastes.

"He called you, too?" Mackenzie asked.

"Yeah," he said. "It looks like we might get our first case together. I figured I'd wait for you before I knocked."

Mackenzie wasn't sure if he had done this out of respect for her or fear of McGrath. Either way, she thought it was a smart decision.

She knocked on the door and was greeted by a quick "Come in" from the other side. She waved Harrison on and they walked into the room together. McGrath was sitting behind his desk, typing something into his laptop. There were two folders sitting to his left, as if waiting to be claimed.

"Have a seat, Agents," he said.

Mackenzie and Harrison each took one of the chairs in front of McGrath's desk. Mackenzie saw that Harrison was sitting rigid and his eyes were wide…not quite with fear but certainly filled with a nervous excitement.

"We've got a case from rural Iowa," he began. "Being that it's where you grew up, I thought you'd be good for this one, White."

She cleared her throat, embarrassed.

"I grew up in Nebraska, sir," she corrected.

"All the same, isn't it?" he said.

She shook her head; those who weren't from the Midwest would just never get it.

*Iowa,* she thought. Sure, it wasn't Nebraska, but it was close enough, and the mere idea of heading back out that way made her uneasy. She knew she had no reason to fear the place; after all, she had made it to Quantico and made something of herself. She had achieved her dream of landing a role in the FBI. So why did the idea of traveling back there for a case unnerve her so quickly?

*Because everything bad in your life is back there,* she thought. *Your childhood, your old colleagues, the mysteries surrounding your father's death…*

"There has been a string of disappearances, all women," McGrath went on. "And so far it seems that they are being taken right off the road on these lonely little stretches of highway. The latest one was taken last night. Her car was found on the side of the road with two busted tires. There was a ridiculous amount of glass on the road, making the local PD assume there was foul play."

He slid one of the folders over to Mackenzie and she took a look. There were several photos of the car, especially the tires. She also saw that the stretch of road was indeed isolated, surrounded by tall trees on both sides. One of the pictures also showed the contents

6

of the latest victim's car. Inside there was a coat, a small toolbox bolted to the side, and a box of books.

"What's with the books?" Mackenzie asked.

"The latest victim was an author. Delores Manning. Google tells me she just had her second book published. One of those trashy romance deals. She's not a big-time author by any means so we shouldn't get any media interference…*yet.* The road has been closed off and detours set up by the state transportation department. So, White, I need you on a plane as soon as possible to get out there. Rural or not, the state obviously doesn't want the road closed down for very long."

McGrath then turned his attention to Harrison.

"Agent Harrison, I want you to understand something. Agent White has ties to the Midwest, so she was a no-brainer for this case. And while I *have* assigned you as her partner, I want you to stay here for this one. I want you here at headquarters to work behind the scenes. If Agent White calls with a research request, I want you on it. Not only that, but Delores Manning has an agent and publicist and all of that. So if this is not wrapped up quickly, the media *will* hop on it. I want you to handle that side of things. Keep things smooth and calm here at headquarters if the shit hits the fan. No offense, but I want a more experienced agent on this."

Harrison nodded, but the disappointment in his eyes was impossible to miss. "No offense taken, sir. I'm happy to assist however I can."

*Oh no,* Mackenzie thought. *Not a brown-noser.*

"So am I going solo on this?" Mackenzie asked.

McGrath grinned at her and shook his head. It was almost a playful kind of gesture that showed her that she had come a long way with McGrath since their first awkward and borderline hostile meetings.

"No way am I sending you out there by yourself," he said. "I've arranged to have Agent Ellington work this one with you."

"Oh," she said, a bit stunned.

She wasn't sure how to feel about this. There was a weird sort of chemistry between her and Ellington—there had been ever since she had first met him while working as a detective out of rural Nebraska. She had enjoyed working with him for that short span but now that things were different…well, it would make for an interesting case to say the least. But there was nothing to worry about. She felt confident that she could easily divide whatever personal feelings she had for him from the professional ones.

"Might I ask why?" Mackenzie asked.

"He's got a brief history of working with the local field agents out there, as you know. He's also got an impressive record when it comes to missing persons cases. Why?"

"Just asking, sir," she said, easily recalling the first time she and Ellington had met when he had come out to assist with the Scarecrow Killer case when she was still working for the PD out there. "Did he...well, did he *ask* to work with me on this?"

"No," McGrath said. "It just so happens that you're both perfect for this case—him with his connections and you with your past."

McGrath stood up from his chair, effectively ending the conversation. "You should be getting e-mails about your flight within a few minutes," McGrath said. "I believe you'll be flying out at eleven fifty-five."

"But that's only an hour and a half away," she said.

"Then I suggest you get moving."

She exited the office quickly, looking back only once to see Agent Harrison still sitting in his seat like a lost puppy, unsure of what to do or where to go. But she had no time to worry about his potentially hurt feelings. She had to figure out how to pack and get to the airport in less than an hour and a half.

And on top of that, she had to figure out why she dreaded the idea of working a case with Ellington.

# CHAPTER TWO

Mackenzie arrived at the airport running, with barely enough time to reach her gate. She rushed onto the plane five minutes after the flight had started to board and ambled down the aisle slightly out of breath, frustrated and thrown off. She briefly wondered if Ellington had made it on time but, quite frankly, was just glad she had not missed the flight. Ellington was a big boy—he could take care of himself.

Her question was answered when she located her seat. Ellington was already on the plane, sitting comfortably in the seat beside hers. He smiled at her from his place by the window seat, giving her a little wave. She shook her head and sighed heavily.

"Bad day?" he asked.

"Well, it started with a funeral and then a meeting with McGrath," Mackenzie said. "I then had to rush home to pack a bag and run through Dulles to barely make the flight. And it's not even noon yet."

"So things can only get better then," Ellington joked.

Shoving her carry-on into the overhead compartment, Mackenzie said: "We'll see. Say, doesn't the FBI have private planes?"

"Yes, but only for extremely time-sensitive cases. And for superstar employees. This case is not time sensitive and we are most certainly not star employees."

When she was finally in her seat, she took a moment to relax. She peered over at Ellington and saw that he was thumbing through a folder that was identical to the one she had seen in McGrath's office.

"What do you think of this case?" Ellington asked.

"I think it's too soon to speculate," she said.

He gave her a roll of his eyes and a playful frown. "You've got to have some sort of first reaction. What is it?"

While she didn't want to offer her thoughts only to be proven wrong later on, she appreciated the effort of jumping on things right away. It showed that he was indeed the hard worker and committed agent McGrath painted him to be—the same kind of worker she had kind of *hoped* he was.

"I think the fact that these are being called *disappearances* rather than *murders* gives us some hope," she said. "But given that the victims are all being taken from rural roads also tells me that this guy is a local that knows the lay of the land. He *could* be kidnapping the women and then killing them, hiding their bodies somewhere in the forests or some other hiding spot only he knows about."

"You read deep into this yet?" he asked, nodding at the folder.

"No. I haven't had time."

"Help yourself," Ellington said, handing it over.

Mackenzie read over the scant information as the flight attendants walked through the safety lecture. She was still studying it moments later when the plane took off toward Des Moines. There wasn't much information in the file, but enough for Mackenzie to map out an approach to take when they got there.

Delores Manning was the third woman to be reported missing in the past nine days. The first woman was a local, reported missing by her daughter. Naomi Nyles, forty-seven years of age, also taken from the side of the road. The second was a Des Moines woman named Crystal Hall. She had a slight record, mostly promiscuous stuff in her youth, but nothing serious. When she was abducted, she had been visiting a local cattle farm in the area. The first case had shown no traces of foul play—just an abandoned car on the side of the road. The second abandoned vehicle had been a small pickup truck with a busted tire. The truck had been discovered in the midst of having its tire changed, the jack still under the axle and the flat propped against the side of the truck.

All three instances appeared to have occurred during the night, sometime between 10 p.m. and 3 a.m. So far, nine days after the first abduction, there was not a single shred of evidence and absolutely zero clues.

As she usually did, Mackenzie scanned the information several times, committing it to memory. It wasn't hard in this case, as there wasn't much to take in. She kept going back to the pictures of the rural settings—the back roads that wound through the forests like a massive snake with nowhere to go.

She also allowed herself to slip into the mind of a killer using those roads and the night as cover. He had to be patient. And because of the darkness, he had to be used to being by himself. Darkness would not concern him. He may even prefer to work in the darkness, not only for the cover but for the sense of solitude and isolation. This guy was probably a loner of some sort. He was taking them from the road, apparently in different stressful situations. Car repair, busted tires. That meant he was probably not in this for the sport of killing. He just wanted the women. But *why?*

And how about the latest victim, Delores Manning? *Maybe she was a local with a past history of the area,* Mackenzie thought.

*Either that or just brave as hell to travel those back roads at such an hour...I don't care how good a shortcut it is, that's pretty reckless.*

She hoped this was the case. She hoped the woman was brave. Because bravery, no matter how staged, could often help people deal with tense situations. It was more than just a badge of honor, but a deep psychological trait that helped people cope. She tried to envision Delores Manning, the up-and-coming writer, winding down those roads at night. Brave or not, it simply wasn't a pretty picture.

When Mackenzie was done, she handed the folder back to Ellington. She looked past him and to the window beyond where white tufts of clouds were drifting by. She closed her eyes for just a moment and took herself back there, not to Iowa but to neighboring Nebraska. A place where there was open land and towering woods rather than mangled traffic and tall buildings. She didn't really miss it but found that the idea of returning to it, even for work, was exciting in a way she did not fully understand.

"White?"

She opened her eyes at the sound of her name. She turned to Ellington, a little embarrassed that he had caught her zoning out. "Yeah?"

"You sort of went blank there for a minute. You okay?"

"I am," she said.

And the hell of it was that she *was* okay. The first six hours of the day had been physically and emotionally draining, but now that she was sitting down, suspended in the air and with an unlikely temporary partner, she felt *okay.*

"Let me ask you something," Mackenzie said.

"Shoot."

"Did you put in a request to work with me on this?"

Ellington didn't answer right away. She could see the cogs turning behind his eyes before he replied and wondered why he might have any reason to lie to her.

"Well, I heard about the case and, as you know, I have a working relationship with the field office in Omaha. And since that's the closest field office to our target in Iowa, I threw my hat in the ring. When he asked if I minded working with you on the case, I didn't argue."

She nodded, starting to feel almost guilty for wondering if he had any other reason for wanting the job. While she had been harboring some sort of feelings for him (whether strictly physical or somehow emotional, she had never been sure), he had never given her any reason to assume he felt the same. It was far too easy to recall coming on to him when she had first met him out in Nebraska and then getting rejected.

*Let's just hope he's forgotten all about that,* she thought. *I'm a different person now, he's far too busy to worry himself with me, and we're working together now. Water under the bridge.*

"So how about you?" she asked. "What are your initial thoughts?"

"I think he has no intention of killing the women," Ellington said. "No clues, no showing off, and, like you, I think it's got to be a local doing it. I think he's maybe collecting them...for what purpose, I won't speculate. But that worries me, if I'm right."

It worried Mackenzie, too. If there was someone out there kidnapping women, he would eventually run out of room. And maybe interest...which meant he'd have to stop sooner or later. And while that was theoretically a good thing, it also meant that his trail would go cold without any further scenes to possibly leave evidence at.

"I think you're right about him collecting them," she said. "He's coming after them in a vulnerable state—while they're messing with cars or busted tires. It means he's sneaking up rather than being in your face. He's likely timid."

He grinned and said, "Huh. That's a good observation."

His grin turned into a smile that she had to look away from, knowing that they had a habit of locking eyes and letting the stares linger a bit too long. Instead, she turned her eyes back out to the blue sky and the clouds while the Midwest quickly approached below them.

***

With very little luggage between them, Mackenzie and Ellington made their way through the airport without any trouble. During the tail end of the flight, Ellington informed Mackenzie that plans had already been made (presumably while she had been rushing to her apartment and then to the airport). She and Ellington were to meet two local field agents and work with them to get the case wrapped up as quickly as possible. With no need to stop by the luggage carousel, they were able to meet with the agents with no problem.

They met in one of the countless Starbucks in the airport. She let Ellington lead the way because it was apparent that McGrath saw him as the lead on the case. Why else would he leave Ellington in charge of knowing where to meet the field agents? Why else would Ellington have been given a proper heads-up, with plenty of time to comfortably make his flight on time?

The two agents were hard to miss. Mackenzie sighed internally when she saw that they were both men. One of them, though, looked like he was brand new. There was no way the guy was any older than twenty-four. His partner looked rather hardened and older—probably reaching fifty any day now.

Ellington headed straight for them and Mackenzie followed. Neither of the agents stood but the older one offered his hand to Ellington as they approached the table.

"Agents Heideman and Thorsson, I take it?" Ellington asked.

"Guilty," the older man said. "I'm Thorsson, and my partner here is Heideman."

"Good to meet you," Ellington said. "I'm Special Agent Ellington and this is my partner, Agent White."

They all shook hands in a way that had become almost tedious to Mackenzie ever since she had joined the bureau. It was almost like a formality, an awkward thing that needed to be done in order to get to the task at hand. She noticed that when Heideman shook her hand, his grip was weak and sweaty. He didn't look nervous but perhaps a bit shy or introverted.

"So how far out are the crime scenes?" Ellington asked. "The closest one is about an hour away," Thorsson said. "The others are all within ten or fifteen minutes of one another."

"Have there been any updates since early this morning?" Mackenzie asked.

"Zero," Thorsson said. "That's one of the reasons we called you guys in. This guy has taken three women so far and we can't generate as much as a single scrap of evidence. It's gotten so bad that the state is considering the use of cameras along the highway. The hurdle there, though, is that you can't really keep over seventy-five miles of back road under surveillance with cameras."

"Well, you technically could," Heideman said. "But that's a ton of cameras and a huge chunk of change. So some folks at the state level are only viewing it as a last-ditch effort."

"Can we go ahead and see the first scene then?" Ellington asked.

"Sure," Thorsson said. "Do you guys need to handle hotels and things like that first?"

"No," Mackenzie said. "Let's get to work for now. If you guys are saying there's *that* much road that needs to be covered, we can't waste any time."

As Thorsson and Heideman stood, Ellington gave her a peculiar look. She couldn't tell if he was impressed with her dedication to get out to the first scene as quickly as possible or if he found it amusing that she wasn't letting him take the *entire* lead on this. What she hoped he couldn't sense was that the thought of going anywhere near a hotel with Ellington made her feel far too many emotions at once.

They left the Starbucks in something of a single file line. Mackenzie was slightly touched when Ellington waited for her, making sure she didn't bring up the back of the line.

"You know," Thorsson said, looking back over his shoulder, "I'm glad you guys want to get out there right away. There's a bad vibe going around about this whole thing. You can feel it when you talk to the local police force and it's starting to rub off on us, too."

"What kind of vibe?" Mackenzie asked.

Thorsson and Heideman shared a foreboding look between them before Thorsson's shoulders slumped a bit and he answered: "Like it's just not going to happen. I've never seen anything like it. There's not a single clue to be had. The guy's like a ghost."

"Well, hopefully we can help with that," Ellington said.

"I hope so," Thorsson said. "Because as of right now, the general feeling among everyone working this case is that we might never find this guy."

# CHAPTER THREE

Mackenzie was rather surprised that the local office had provided Thorsson and Heideman with a Suburban. After her own clunker and the template rental cars she'd been stuck with over the past few months, she felt like she was traveling in style while sitting in the back with Ellington. When they arrived at the first scene an hour and ten minutes later, she was almost glad to be out of it, though. She wasn't used to such nice perks with her position and it made her feel a little uncomfortable.

Thorsson parked along the edge of State Route 14, a basic two-lane back road that wound through the forests of rural Iowa. The road was bordered with trees on both sides. During the few miles they had been on this road, Mackenzie had seen a few small dirt roads that seemed to have been long forgotten, chained off by a thin cable and two posts on either side of the tracks. Other than those few breaks, there was nothing more than trees.

Thorsson and Heideman led them past a few local cops who gave perfunctory waves as they passed. Up ahead, in front of two parked police cars, was a little red Subaru. The two driver's side tires were completely flat.

"What's the police force like around here?" Mackenzie asked.

"Small," Thorsson said. "The nearest town to here is a little place called Bent Creek. Population of about nine hundred. The police force consists of one sheriff—who is back there with those other guys—two deputies, and seven officers. They had a few suits from Des Moines come in but when we showed up, they stepped back. It's the FBI's problem now. That kind of thing."

"So they're glad we're here, in other words?" Ellington asked.

"Oh, absolutely," Thorsson said.

They approached the car and all circled it for a moment. Mackenzie took a look back at the officers. Only one of them seemed legitimately interested in what the visiting FBI agents were doing. As far as she was concerned, that was fine with her. She'd had her fair share of meddling small-town police officers making things harder than they had to be. It would be nice to work a job without having to tiptoe around the sensitivities and egos of the local PD.

"Has the car already been dusted for prints?" Mackenzie asked.

"Yeah, earlier this morning," Heideman said. "Help yourself."

Mackenzie opened the passenger side door. A brief look around told her that while the vehicle might have been dusted for prints, nothing had yet been removed and tagged as evidence. A cell phone still sat in the passenger seat. A pack of gum sat on top of a few scattered and folded pieces of paper in the center console.

"This is the author's car, correct?" Mackenzie asked.

"It is," Thorsson said. "Delores Manning."

Mackenzie continued checking the car. She found Manning's sunglasses, a mostly empty address book, a few copies of *The Tin House* scattered in the back seat, and spare change here and there. The trunk offered only a box of books. There were eighteen copies of a book called *Love Blocked* by Delores Manning.

"Was everything back here dusted for prints?" Mackenzie asked.

"No, I don't think so," Heideman said. "It's just a box of books, right?"

"Yes, but some are missing."

"She came from a signing," Thorsson said. "Chances are pretty good she sold some or gave some away."

It wasn't anything worth arguing about so she let it go. Still, Mackenzie flipped through two of the books. They had both been signed by Manning on the title page.

She put the books back into the box and then started to study the road. She walked along the edge, looking for any indentations where something might have been set up that would have flattened the tires. She looked over to Ellington and was pleased to see that he was already studying the flats. From where she stood, she could see the glittering shards of glass still sticking out of the tires.

There was more of the glass in the road ahead. The bit of sunlight that managed to break through the tree branches overhead bounced off of them in a way that was eerily pretty. She walked over to it and squatted down for a better look.

It was obvious that the glass had been placed there intentionally. It was located primarily close to the broken yellow lines in the center of the road. It was scattered here and there like sand but the main concentration had been spaced out to ensure that anyone driving along would run directly over it. A few larger shards remained in the road; the car had apparently missed these, as they had not been ground down into crumb-like bits. She picked up one of these larger pieces and studied it.

The glass was dark at first glance but as Mackenzie took a closer look, she saw that it had been painted black. *To kill the glare of approaching headlights,* she thought. *Someone driving at night would see glass in their headlights ... but not if it was painted black.*

16

She selected a few pieces from the debris and scratched at a few larger pieces with her fingernail. The glass underneath was two different colors; most of it was clear but some of it had a very slight green tint to it. It was far too thick to be from any sort of drinking bottle or common jar. It had the thickness of something that a potter might make. Some if it looked to be easily as much as an inch and a half in width even after it had been broken and then shattered by Delores Manning's car.

"Anyone notice that this glass has been spray-painted?" she asked.

Along the side of the road, the officers were looking to one another as if confused. Even Thorsson and Heideman gave one another a quizzical look.

"That's a *no*," Thorsson said.

"Has any of it been bagged and analyzed yet?" Mackenzie asked.

"Bagged, yes," Thorsson said. "Analyzed, no. But there's a team on it right now. We should have some sort of results in a few hours. I guess they would have eventually gotten back to us on the spray paint."

"And this glass was not at any of the other scenes, is that correct?"

"That's right."

Mackenzie got to her feet, looking down at the glass as she started to paint a picture of the kind of suspect they might be looking for.

*No glass at the previous scenes,* she thought. *That means the suspect was purposeful about this one woman. Why? Maybe the first two disappearances were just coincidence. Maybe the subject just happened to be in the right place at the right time. And if that was the case, he's definitely a local—a rural killer, not an urban one. But he's smart and calculated. He's not just doing his tasks by the seat of his pants.*

Ellington came over to her and inspected the glass for himself. Without looking up at her, he asked: "Any initial thoughts?"

"A few."

"Such as?"

"He's a rural guy. Likely a local, as we thought. I also think this one was planned. The flat tires...he did it on purpose. If the glass was not present at the other scenes, he set it out only this time. It makes me think he had no control over the other two. It was just luck on his part. But this one...this one he had to work for."

"You think it's worth speaking to family?" Ellington asked.

She could not tell if he was quizzing her in some weird way like Bryers had once done or if he was genuinely interested in her methodology and approach.

"Might be the fastest way to get any answers for right now," she said. "Even if it nets nothing, it's a task completed."

"That sounds like a robot talking," Ellington said with a smile.

Ignoring him, Mackenzie walked back over to the car where Thorsson and Heideman had been watching them.

"Do we know where Delores Manning lives?" she asked.

"Well, she lives in Buffalo, New York," Thorsson said. "But she has family out near Sigourney."

"That's in Iowa, too, right?"

"It is," Thorsson said. "Her mother lives about ten minutes outside of the town. Father is deceased. No one has informed them of her disappearance yet. From what we can tell, she's only been missing for twenty-six hours or so. And while we can't confirm it, we can't help but wonder if she paid her family a visit while she was so close because of her book signing in Cedar Rapids."

"I think they should probably be informed," Mackenzie said.

"Same here," Ellington said, joining them.

"Be my guest, then," Thorsson chuckled. "Sigourney is about an hour and fifteen minutes away. We'd love to tag along," he added sarcastically, "but that wasn't in our orders."

As he said this, one of the policemen joined them. The badge he wore indicated that this was the sheriff of the area.

"You need us around for anything?" he asked.

"Nope," Ellington said. "Maybe just the name of a decent hotel around here."

"There's only one back in Bent Creek," the sheriff said. "So that's the only one I can really recommend."

"Well then, it looks like we'll take your recommendation. And we'll also need one for a rental car in Bent Creek."

"I can get you fixed up," the sheriff said, leaving it at that.

With a slight sense of feeling displaced, Mackenzie walked back to the Suburban and took her place in the back seat. As the three other agents piled in, Mackenzie started to think about those little dirt tracks off of State Route 14. Who owned that property? Where did the roads lead?

As they headed toward Bent Creek, the country roads seemed to present more and more questions in Mackenzie's mind...some menial but some very pressing. She collected them all as she thought about the broken glass in the road. She tried to imagine someone painting that glass with the clear intention of causing someone's car to break down.

It spoke of more than just intent. It indicated careful planning and knowing the flow of traffic along State Route 14 at that time of night.

*Our guy is smart in a dangerous sort of way,* she thought. *He's also a planner and seems to be going after women only.*

She started to put a profile together for such a suspect and instantly started to feel a sense of pressure...of the need to move quickly. She felt he was somewhere within this little rural hole of trees and winding roads, breaking up more glass, spraying it with spray paint.

And planning to capture another victim.

# CHAPTER FOUR

Delores Manning was thinking of her mother when she opened her eyes. Her mother, who lived in a shit-kicking mobile home park just outside of Sigourney. The woman was very proud, very stubborn. The plan had been for Delores to visit her after the signing in Cedar Rapids. Having just signed a contract for a three-book deal with her current publisher, Delores had written a check for $7,000, hoping her mother would take it and use it wisely. Maybe it was snobby, but Delores was embarrassed that her mother was on welfare, that she had to use food stamps to buy groceries. It had been that way since her father died and—

The foggy thoughts of her mother drifted off as her eyes started to grow accustomed to the darkness she found herself in. She was sitting down with her back pressed against something very hard and almost cool to the touch. Slowly, she got to her feet. When she did, she struck her head on something that felt exactly like the surface against her back.

Confused, she reached up and could not extend her arms very far at all. As panic started to creep in, her eyes realized that there were tiny slats of light falling into the darkness. Directly in front of her were three rectangular bars of light. The bars alone filled her in on her situation.

She was in some kind of container...she was pretty sure it was made of steel or some other kind of metal. The container was no more than four feet tall, not allowing her to fully stand. It seemed to be no deeper than four feet and about the same width. She started to take shallow breaths, instantly feeling claustrophobic.

She pressed herself against the front wall of the container and drew in fresh air through the rectangular slats. Each slat was roughly six inches tall and maybe three inches across. When she drew in the air through her nose, she detected an earthy smell and something sweet yet unpleasant.

Somewhere further off in the distance, so faint it may as well have been on another world, she thought she heard a sort of squealing noise. Machinery? Maybe some type of animal? Yes, an animal...but she had no idea what kind. Pigs, maybe?

With her breaths coming more naturally now, she took a step back in her crouched position and then peered through the slats.

Outside, she saw what looked to be the interior of a barn or some other old wooden building. Perhaps twenty feet ahead of her, she could see the door to the barn. Murky sunlight came in through the warped frame where the door did not set flush against it. While she could not see much, she saw enough to gauge that she was probably in very serious trouble.

It was evident in the edge of the bolted door she could just barely see through the slats of the container. She whimpered and pushed against the front of the container. There was no give—not so much as a creaking noise.

She felt panic creeping up again so knew she'd have to use the little bit of logic and calmness she now possessed. She ran her hands along the bottom of the container's door. She was hoping to find hinges, maybe something with screws or bolts that she could potentially work on. She wasn't very strong, but if even one screw was either loose or crooked...

Again, there was nothing. She tried the same thing on the back and found nothing there as well.

In an act of absolute helplessness, she kicked at the door as hard as she could. When that did no good, she went to the back of the container and got a running start to throw her right shoulder into it. All that accomplished was having her rebound and fall backward. She hit her head on the side of the container and fell hard to her backside.

A scream rose up in her throat but she didn't know if that would be the best thing to do. She could easily recall the man from the truck on the road and how he had attacked her. Did she *really* want him to come rushing to her?

No, she did not. *Think,* she told herself. *Use that creative brain of yours and figure a way out of this.*

But she could think of nothing. So, while she was able to choke down the scream that wanted to come out, she was unable to hold back the tears. She kicked at the front of the container and then fell into the back corner. She wept as quietly as she could, rocking back and forth in a seated position and looking to the shafts of dusty light that spilled in through the slats.

For now, it was all she could think to do.

# CHAPTER FIVE

Mackenzie did not like the fact that her mind brought up dozens of clichéd stereotypes as she and Ellington pulled into the entrance of the Sigourney Oaks Mobile Home Court. The mobile homes were all dusty and looked to be on their last legs. The vehicles parked in front of most of them were in the same shape. In the dead yard of one of the trailers they passed, two men sat shirtless in lawn chairs. A cooler of beer rested between them, as well as several empty and crushed cans…at 4:35 in the afternoon.

The home of Tammy Manning, Delores Manning's mother, was located directly in the middle of the park. Ellington parked the rental car behind a beaten up old Chevy pickup. The rental car looked better than the vehicles in the park, but not by much. The selection at Smith Brothers Auto had been meager and they had ended up selecting a 2008 Ford Fusion that was in dire need of a paint job and a new set of tires.

As they walked up the rickety front steps to the door, Mackenzie made a quick sweep of the place. A few kids were rolling toy cars along in the dirt. A pre-teen girl walked blindly with her eyes glued to a cell phone, her belly exposed through the dirty shirt she wore. An old man two trailers down was lying on the ground, peering up under a lawnmower with a wrench in his hand and oil on his pants.

Ellington knocked on the door and it was answered almost instantly. The woman that answered the door was pretty in a plain way. She looked to be in her fifties and the strands of gray in her otherwise black hair stood out in a way that was almost like decoration rather than the signs of age. She looked tired but the smell that came off of her breath when she said "Who are you?" made Mackenzie pretty sure that she'd been drinking.

Ellington answered but made sure not to step in front of Mackenzie when he did so. "I'm Agent Ellington and this is Agent White, with the FBI," he said.

"FBI?" she asked. "What the hell for?"

"Are you Tammy Manning?" he asked.

"I am," she said.

"Can we come in?" Ellington asked.

Tammy eyed them in a way that was not suspicious but something closer to disbelief. She nodded and stepped back, allowing them in. The moment they walked inside, the thick smell of cigarette smoke engulfed them. The air was filled with it. A lone cigarette burned in an ashtray of dead butts on an old coffee table.

Another woman sat on the couch on the opposite side of the coffee table. She looked a little uncomfortable. Mackenzie thought she actually appeared a little grossed out to be sitting there.

"If you have company," Mackenzie said, "perhaps we should speak outside."

"She's not company," Tammy said. "This is my daughter Rita."

"Hi," Rita said, standing to shake their hands.

It was apparent that this was Delores Manning's younger sister by about three or four years. She looked very similar to the photo of Delores that Mackenzie had seen on the back cover of *Love Blocked.*

"Oh, I see," Ellington said. "Well, maybe it's a good thing that you're here too, Rita."

"Why?" Tammy asked, plopping down next to her younger daughter. She plucked the cigarette from the ashtray and took a deep inhale.

"Delores Manning's car was discovered abandoned with two flat tires on State Route 14 late last night. No one has seen her or heard from her since then. Not her agent, not any friends, no one. We were hoping you might know where she is."

Before Ellington was done, Mackenzie had gotten the answer from the look of shock on Rita Manning's face.

"Oh my God," Rita said. "Are you sure it was her car?"

"We're certain," Ellington said. "It was complete with half a box of her latest book in the back. She had just come from a signing in Cedar Rapids."

"Yeah," Rita said. "She was…probably on the way here. That was the plan anyway. When she didn't show up by midnight, I figured she just decided to stay at a motel somewhere."

"Had you made plans for her to stay here?" Mackenzie asked. She was looking at Tammy when she asked it, but Tammy appeared to be more interested in enjoying her cigarette.

"Sort of," Tammy said. "She called me last week and said she'd be in Cedar Rapids. Said she wanted to come by to visit, so I told her that was fine. I let Rita know and she got here yesterday right after lunch. Sort of a surprise."

"I drove all the way up from Texas A and M," Rita said.

"When was the last time you spoke with Delores?" Ellington asked Rita.

"About three weeks ago. We usually do an okay job of staying in touch."

"What state of mind was she in the last time you spoke?" Mackenzie asked.

"Oh, she was on cloud nine. She had just signed on to do another three books with her publisher. We made plans to go out on the town drinking the next time she was in Texas."

"You're a student, I take it?" Ellington asked.

"Yes. A senior."

"Mrs. Manning," Mackenzie said, making sure the mother knew that she was being spoken to and not the daughter, "if you don't mind my saying so, you don't seem too bothered by this."

She shrugged, exhaled a mouthful of smoke, and then ground the butt out in the overflowing ashtray. "I guess someone from the FBI knows more about how I should feel about something like this than I do?"

"I wasn't saying that, ma'am," Mackenzie said.

"Look...we're talking about Delores here. She's got a good head on her shoulders. I'm sure she called Triple A or some shit when the tires went flat. She's probably already halfway back to New York by now. Making money, traveling the country. If she was in some kind of trouble, she would have called."

"So she wouldn't have been embarrassed to call for your help?"

Tammy actually thought about this for a minute. "Probably not. She would have called for help and then raised hell if I asked even one question. It's just how she is."

The resentment in her voice was almost as thick as the smoke in the air throughout the tiny trailer.

"So you have no idea where she might be?" Ellington asked.

"None. Wherever she is, she didn't bother calling me to tell me about it. But that's not too big of a surprise. She never really tells me much of anything."

"I see," Ellington said. He looked around the room with a frown. Mackenzie could tell that he was thinking the same thing she was thinking: *That was a wasted hour-and-ten-minute drive.*

Mackenzie looked directly toward Rita, currently a little pissed at the lack of help from Tammy. "We've got Bent Creek PD on it, as well as agents from two different offices. From what we know, she's been missing for roughly twenty-nine hours. We'll be in touch the moment we find anything."

Rita gave a nod and a soft "Thank you."

Both Mackenzie and Ellington paused a beat to give Tammy a chance to add anything. When she did nothing more than light up another cigarette and reach for the TV remote on the coffee table, Mackenzie headed for the door.

When she was outside, she breathed the fresh air in deeply and walked straight for the car. She was already opening the passenger side door when Ellington finally made it down the steps.

"You okay?" he asked her as he approached the car.

"I'm fine," she said. "I just can't stomach people that have no concern at all for the safety of their own flesh and blood."

She was about to get into the car when the front door of Tammy Manning's trailer opened. They both watched as Rita came down the stairs in a quick little jog. She came over to the car and let out a shaky sigh.

"Oh my God, I'm so sorry about that," she said. Mackenzie saw that Rita also seemed to be breathing much easier now that she was outside. "Things with Mom and Delores haven't been the best ever since Dad died. And then when Delores became this well-to-do writer, something about it almost offended Mom."

"You don't have to explain personal problems," Ellington said. "We see it from time to time."

"Be honest with me...this thing with Delores...do you think she'll be found? Do you think she might be dead somewhere?"

"It's far too early to tell," Mackenzie said.

"Was it...well, was there anything like foul play?"

Mackenzie recalled the spray-painted glass. She was pretty sure she still had some of the black flakes of the paint under her fingernails. But it was far too soon in the course of events to give such information to family members—not until more information could be obtained.

"Again, we just can't know for sure yet," she said.

Rita nodded. "Well, thanks for letting us know. When you *do* find out anything, just call me directly. Forget about Mom for now. I don't know what her problem is. She's just...I don't know. An aging woman that let life beat the hell out of her and never bothered to pick herself back up."

She gave them her number and then slowly walked back up the stairs. She gave them a quick wave goodbye as Ellington backed out of the parking spot and headed back through the trailer park.

"So what do you think?" Ellington asked. "Was this a wasted trip?"

"No. I think we now know enough about Delores to know that she would have called if her plans changed and she *could* have called."

"How do you know that for sure?"

"I don't know *for sure*. But from what I gathered from Tammy and Rita, Delores was trying to reconnect with her family. Rita said

25

there was a strained relationship there. I don't think Delores would have bothered calling to ask to come by for a visit if there was no hope for reconciliation. And if that's the case, she surely would have called if plans changed."

"Maybe she had a change of heart."

"I doubt it. Daughters and mothers...when they get estranged...it's tough. Delores would not have made the move of calling only to back out."

"You're analyzing this like a shrink," Ellington said. "That's impressive."

Mackenzie barely noticed the compliment. She was thinking about her own mother—a woman she had not spoken to in a very long time. It was easy to strain a relationship that was supposed to be so pivotal to a woman's life. She knew all about mothers who let their children down, so she could relate to Delores.

She wondered if Delores Manning was thinking of her mother in her desperate time. That was, of course, if Delores Manning was still alive.

# CHAPTER SIX

Mackenzie knew that the closest FBI field office to Bent Creek was in Omaha, Nebraska. The thought of returning to Nebraska in an official capacity was intimidating, yet at the same time, almost fitting. Still, she was beyond relieved when Heideman called them to let them know that the current base of operations for the case was in the Bent Creek police department.

She and Ellington arrived there just after six that evening. As she walked toward the front doors of the station with Ellington, feelings of working as a woman in law enforcement in the Midwest came creeping back in. It was in the nearly misogynistic way some of the men in uniform looked at her. The change of clothes and title had apparently done nothing. Men were still going to see her as second class.

The only difference now was that she didn't give a shit if she offended anyone or hurt their feelings. She was here on bureau business to help a small and fledgling police force figure out who was kidnapping women from their back roads. She was not going to be treated the same way she had been the last time she worked in the Midwest as a detective for the Nebraska State Police.

She quickly discovered that part of her assumptions upon entering the station were wrong. Maybe the change of title and stature *did* mean something. When they were escorted back to the primary conference room, she saw that the local PD had ordered Chinese food for them. It was spread out on a small coffee bar in the back of the room, along with a few two-liter bottles of drinks and snacks.

Thorsson and Heideman were already enjoying the comped dinner, shoveling portions of lo mein noodles and orange chicken onto their plates. Ellington gave her a *what are ya gonna do?* sort of shrug and headed for the table as well. She did the same as a few other people filtered in and out of the room. While she was sitting down at the conference table with a portion of sesame chicken and a crab rangoon, one of the officers she had seen on the side of State Route 14 approached her and extended his hand. Again, she saw his badge and recognized him as the sheriff.

"Agent White, right?" he asked.

"I am."

"Good to meet you. I'm Sheriff Bateman. I hear you and your partner went up near Sigourney to talk to the mother of the most recent victim. No results?"

"Nothing. Just a potential source of information to cross off the list. And a pretty good confirmation that we're not dealing with a case of a daughter that simply decided not to call her mother when plans changed."

Clearly disappointed by this, Bateman nodded and turned back for the front of the room where two other officers were in conversation.

As Ellington took a seat beside Mackenzie, they both looked to the front of the room. A man who had earlier introduced himself as Deputy Wickline was placing pictures and printouts on a dry erase board with magnets. Another officer—the only other female in the room—was writing a series of notes along the other side of the board.

"Looks like they run a tight ship around here," Ellington said.

She had been thinking the same thing. She had come in assuming this would be something of a sloppily put together circus as it had been with the Nebraska State PD when she had worked there. But so far, she was impressed with how the Bent Creek PD was organizing things.

Several minutes later, Sheriff Bateman checked in with the officers at the board and ushered the two male officers out. The female stayed behind and took a seat at the table. Bateman closed the door and went to the front of the room. He glanced around at the four FBI agents and three remaining officers in the room.

"We got dinner because I have no idea how long we'll be here," he said. "We don't generally get a lot of bureau presence in Bent Creek so this is new to me. So please, Agents, let me know if there is anything we can do to make things smoother. For now, I'll turn this over to you agents."

He took a seat, leaving Ellington and Thorsson to give one another a quick confused look. Thorsson grinned and gestured to the front of the room, giving the responsibility to the agents from DC.

Ellington nudged Mackenzie lightly under the table as he said: "Yes, so Agent White will walk us through the information we have so far, as well as any current theories we have."

She knew he was trying to rib her by throwing her under the bus in such a way, but she didn't mind. In fact, a small selfish part of her wanted to be in front of the room. Maybe it was some girlish revenge fantasy to come back to this area of the country and run a conference room in a way she had never been allowed to do in Nebraska. Whatever the reason, she went to the front of the room and took a quick look at the dry erase board that had been put together.

"The work your officers did here," she said, pointing to the board, "pretty much spells the story out for me. The first victim is a resident of Bent Creek. Naomi Nyles, forty-seven years of age. She was reported missing by her daughter and was last seen two weeks ago. Her car was found on the side of the road in no apparent state of disrepair. I believe officers within this very building were able to crank the car just fine and bring it back here."

"That's correct," Deputy Wickline said. "The car is still in the impound lot, as a matter of fact."

"The second missing person was twenty-six-year-old Crystal Hall. Her employer is Wrangler Beef in Des Moines and they have confirmed that she was sent to a cattle farm just outside of Bent Creek. The owner of the farm confirms that Crystal did show up for a planned meeting and left the property shortly after five in the afternoon. Her credit card history shows that she grabbed dinner at the Bent Creek Subway at five fifty-two." She pointed to where one of the helpful officers had already jotted this information down on the board.

"The question that raises," Bateman said, "is when she was abducted. Her car was not discovered until around one thirty in the morning. For someone to not notice her car or at least report it, even on State Route 14, means that there's a good chance she was elsewhere in town before heading back home. I seriously doubt someone would have been bold enough to nab her between six thirty and seven thirty. And if they *were* that bold..."

He trailed off here, as if not liking how he needed to end the comment. So Mackenzie took the liberty and finished for him.

"Then it means it would be someone familiar with the area," she said. "Particularly with the traffic patterns on State Route 14. However, the profile for this type of guy doesn't line up with being so bold. He lurks in darkness. He sneaks up on them. There's nothing at all overt about this guy."

Bateman nodded at this, his eyes wide and a smile on his face. She'd seen the look before. It was the look of a man who was not only impressed by the way she thought, but *appreciated* it. She saw the same look on the face of the female officer and an overweight man at the end of the table, still enjoying the free dinner. Deputy Wickline was nodding at her comment, scribbling notes down in a legal pad.

"Sheriff," Ellington said, "do we have any idea the average amount of traffic that goes through that route at that time of day?"

"A state-sanctioned traffic monitor and report from 2012 estimates that between six in the afternoon and midnight, there's an average of about eighty vehicles that will pass through State Route 14. It really isn't a very busy road. But keep in mind, it's just been the author and Crystal Hall that were taken from 14. The first missing person, Naomi Nyles, was abducted off of County Road 664."

"And what's the traffic like there during that time of day?" Mackenzie asked.

"Almost nothing," Bateman said. "I think the number was around twenty or thirty. Deputy Wickline, do you know any different?"

"Sounds about right," Wickline said.

"And speaking of the author," Mackenzie continued. "Delores Manning, thirty-two. She lives in Buffalo but has family just outside of Sigourney. Her tires were flattened by broken glass fragments in the road. The glass is quite thick and had been painted black to prevent glare and shine from the headlights. Her agent reported her as missing about half an hour after her car was discovered by a passing truck around two in the morning. Agent Ellington and I spoke with her mother and sister today and they could provide no solid leads. As a matter of fact, there seem to be no solid leads at all to any of these disappearances. And unfortunately, that's all we have."

"Thank you, Agent White," Bateman said. "So where do we go from here?"

Mackenzie smirked a bit and nodded to the Chinese food on the back table. "Well, it's a good thing you planned ahead. I think the best place to start is to go over any unsolved disappearances within a one-hundred-mile radius over the last ten years."

No one objected but the looks on the faces of Bateman, Wickline, and the other officers said enough. The female officer shrugged in defeat and raised her hand dutifully. "I can get on records and pull all of that," she said.

"Sounds good, Roberts," Bateman said. "Can you have results for us in an hour? Get some of the desk-riders out front to help."

Roberts got up and left the conference room. Mackenzie noticed that Bateman watched her a bit longer than the other men in the room.

"Agent White," Bateman said. "Do you happen to have any ideas as to what kind of suspect we should be looking for? In a fairly small town like Bent Creek, the quicker we can rule people out, the quicker we can point you to the sort of person you're looking for."

"Without clues of any kind, it could be hard to pinpoint," Mackenzie said. "But so far, there are a few certain things we can assume. Agent Ellington, would you like to take over on this part?"

He smiled at her as he took a bite out of an egg roll. "Please, keep going. You're doing just fine."

It was an odd back-and-forth between them that she hoped wasn't too obvious to others in the room. She had been trying to show respect—to show him that she was not trying to run the show. But he, in turn, had shrugged it off. For now, it seemed that he almost appreciated the fact that she was assuming the lead.

"First of all," she said, doing her best not to be thrown off course, "the suspect is almost certainly a local. His ability to study traffic patterns along these back roads shows a rigorous kind of patience that makes him a bit easier to profile. If the suspect has gone through this much trouble to abduct these women, then past cases involving kidnapping and abduction suggest that he is not taking these women to kill them. As I said, he seems to be sneaky. Everything we know about him—attacking when they are vulnerable, in the dark, and apparently planning the act—points to a man with non-violent tendencies. After all, what's the point of painstakingly plotting an abduction only to kill the victim moments later? It indicates that he is *collecting* these women, for lack of a better term."

"Yes," Roberts, the female officer, said. "But collecting them for what, exactly?"

"Is it terrible to assume it's a sex thing?" Deputy Wickline asked.

"Not at all," Mackenzie said. "In fact, if our suspect *is* shy, that's one more check mark on the profile for us. Shy men that go after women in such a way are usually too shy or otherwise burdened socially to romance women. It's usually the case with rapists that do everything they can to not hurt the women."

She got a few more of those admiring glances from around the room. But given the topic that was being discussed, she couldn't appreciate it.

"But we can't know for sure?" Bateman asked.

"No," Mackenzie said. "And that's where the pressure is on us. This isn't just a killer that we are hoping won't strike again. This man is psychotic, and dangerous. The longer it takes to find him, the longer he has to do whatever he wants with these women."

# CHAPTER SEVEN

Filled with Chinese food and an abundance of information on the three abductees, Mackenzie and Ellington left the Bent Creek PD at 9:15. The only motel in town—a Motel 6 that looked like it hadn't been painted, decorated, or looked at twice since the '80s—was five minutes away. It was no surprise at all to find two vacant rooms, which they booked for the night.

When they left the office and stepped back out into the night, Mackenzie looked around the parking lot. Bent Creek truly was a very small town. It was so small, in fact, that the business owners apparently worked together to ensure an efficient use of space. This was evident in the fact that a small bar sat on the other side of the parking lot from the Motel 6. It made sense, Mackenzie thought. Anyone that needed to stay in a motel in Bent Creek was likely going to need a drink.

She certainly could go for one.

Ellington patted her on the back and started in that direction. "Drinks are on me," he said.

She was starting to enjoy the dry and rather basic humor that existed between them. They both knew that there was a shifting awkwardness between them but it had been buried. To get around it, they had created a tentative friendship based on their jobs—jobs that insisted they think logically and approach things with a no-nonsense attitude. So far, it was working quite well.

She joined him as they crossed the parking lot and when they stepped inside the bar—unoriginally named Bent Creek Bar—the gloom of the night was replaced by a smoky and dank sort of twilight that only existed in small-town bars and honkytonks. An old Travis Tritt song was playing on a dusty jukebox in the corner as they took a seat at the edge of the bar. They both ordered beers and, as if that staple of a bar visit had been their cue, Ellington somehow went straight back into work mode.

"I think those offshoot roads off of State Road 14 are worth looking into," he said.

"Same here," she said. "I find it odd that it wasn't mentioned in any of the copious notes the police put up on that board."

"Maybe they just know the geography of the place better than we do," Ellington suggested. "For all we know, they could just be little dirt tracks that dead end. Any reason you didn't ask about them while you were running the conference room?"

"I almost did," she said. "But they'd put it all together so well...I didn't want to step on any toes. This whole thing of a cooperative police department bending over backwards for us is new to me. I'll get to it tomorrow. If it was crucial or important, they've either already checked them or they would have at least mentioned it to us."

Ellington nodded and took a gulp of his beer. "Hell, I nearly forgot," he said. "I was sorry as hell to hear about Bryers. I only worked with him a few times and it wasn't in a close capacity. But he seemed to be a genuinely nice man. One hell of an agent, too, from what I hear."

"Yeah, he was pretty awesome," Mackenzie said.

"I don't know if you'd want to know this or not," Ellington said, "but there was quite a bit of controversy about pairing you with him when you came in. Bryers was something of a hot commodity. One of the best. But when the idea was given to him, he was all for it. I think deep down, he always wanted to be a mentor. And I think he got a good one for his first try."

"Thanks," she said. "But I don't quite feel as if I've proven myself just yet."

"Why not?"

"Well...I don't know. Maybe it will hit me when I can wrap a case without getting McGrath pissed off at me over some detail or another."

"He only does it because he expects so much out of you. You came in like this fuse on a stick of dynamite that had already been lit."

"Is that why he has me partnering with you right now?"

"No. I think he just wanted me on this because of my connection with the Omaha field office. And between you and me and no one else, he wants you to succeed on this one. He wants you to knock it out of the park. With me on board, you won't be able to resort to one of your patented solo endings that you're so prone to."

She wanted to argue this point but she knew he was right. So instead, she drank from her beer. The jukebox was now churning out Bryan Adams and somehow, she was ordering her second beer.

"So tell me," Mackenzie said. "If I wasn't on this one with you, how would you be handling it? What approaches?"

"Same as you. Working closely with the PD and trying to make friends. Taking notes, coming up with theories."

"And do you have any?" she asked.

"None that you didn't already nail in that conference room. I'm thinking we're onto something...thinking of this guy as a collector of sorts. A bashful loner. I feel pretty safe in saying he's not getting these women just to kill them. I think you're exactly right on all those points."

"The thing that gets under my skin," Mackenzie said, "is thinking of all of the other reasons he would be kidnapping and collecting women."

"Did you notice that Sheriff Bateman kept a female officer in the room the whole time?" Ellington asked.

"Yeah. Roberts. I assumed it was to keep the conversation centered on the facts and not speculations. Speculations regarding why the suspect would be keeping women. Talking about rape and sexual abuse is a little easier when there isn't a woman around."

"That kind of stuff bother you?" Ellington asked.

"It used to. Sadly, I've gotten almost jaded about it. It doesn't bother me anymore." This wasn't one hundred percent true, but she didn't want Ellington to know it. The truth of the matter was that it was often things like these that drove her to be the absolute best she could be.

"Sucks, doesn't it?" he asked. "That part of your humanity that sort of becomes numb to things like this?"

"Yeah, it does," she said. She hid herself behind her beer for a moment, a little shocked that Ellington had just taken such a step. It had been a small step for him but it also showed a degree of vulnerability.

She finished her beer and slid it to the edge of the bar. When the bartender came over, she waved him off. "I'm good," she said. Then, turning to Ellington, she said: "You said you were paying, right?"

"Yeah, I got it. Hold on a second and I'll walk you to your room."

The slight excitement she felt at this comment was embarrassing. To stop it in its tracks before she could even entertain it, she shook her head. "Not necessary," she said. "I can take care of myself."

"I know you can," he said, sliding his own empty glass toward the edge of the bar. "Another for me," he told the bartender.

Mackenzie waved to him as she made her way out. As she walked across the parking lot, that small and eager part of her couldn't help but wonder what it might be like to walk back to the motel with Ellington by her side, pushed forward by the uncertainty that would await them once the doors were closed and the blinds were drawn.

It took less than twenty minutes for the sting of lust to subside. As usual, she used work to distract herself from such lures. She opened up her laptop and went directly to her e-mail. There, she found several e-mails that had been sent to her by the Bent Creek PD over the last half a day or so—just another way they were starting to spoil her, really.

They had provided maps of the area, the only four missing persons reports within the area over the last ten years, the traffic analysis conducted by the state of Iowa in 2012, and even a list of all arrests made in the last five years that involved subjects with a history of assault. Mackenzie pored through it all, taking a bit of extra time to look at the four missing persons cases.

Two of them were assumed to have been runaways and after reading the reports, Mackenzie agreed. They could both be used as a template for angst-ridden teenagers who were tired of small-town life, leaving home earlier than their parents would have liked. One of them was a fourteen-year-old girl who had actually contacted her family two years ago to let them know she was living quite comfortably in Los Angeles.

The other two were a little harder to understand, though. One case involved a ten-year-old boy who had been abducted from a church playground. He'd been missing for three hours before anyone even raised much of a fuss about it. Local gossip mills suggested it was the grandmother who took him because of a hairy family situation. The family drama, plus the gender and age of the victim, made Mackenzie doubt there was any connection to the current kidnappings.

The fourth case was more promising but still seemed a little thin. The first red flag was that it involved a car accident. In 2009, Sam and Vicki McCauley had been run off of the road during an ice storm. When police and the ambulance arrived, Sam was barely alive and died on the way to the hospital. He had begged to know how his wife was. From what they could tell, Vicki McCauley had been thrown from the vehicle, but her body had never been found.

Mackenzie looked through the report twice and could not find any descriptions of what had caused the car to leave the road. The term *icy road conditions* was used several times and while that was a good reason, Mackenzie thought it might be a good idea to go deeper. She went through the report several times and then reread Delores Manning's report. The fact that there was a car accident of some kind seemed to be the only connection between the two.

She then shifted gears and tried to weave the current three victims into those scenarios. It was nearly impossible, though. The two unexplained cases were assumed runaways and while both were female, it left far too many options open. More than that, the three current victims were taken from their cars. Maybe because being stranded on the road was a fairly common occurrence. It was a far cry from nabbing a teenage runaway. It simply didn't fit.

*This guy doesn't want runaways or troubled teens that storm out to get a rise out of mom and dad. He's going after women. Women that are, for some reason or another, out in their cars at night. Maybe he realizes the hope that the apparent kind stranger instills in people—women especially.*

On the flip side of that, though, was the fact that she knew most women would assume the worst of a strange man on the side of the road. Especially when their cars were busted and it was dark.

*Maybe they know him, then…*

That seemed like a stretch, too. From the information they had gathered from Tammy and Rita Manning, Delores likely didn't know anyone in Bent Creek.

She went back to the McCauleys' case, mainly because it was the only one with even the thinnest thread of similarity to it. She pulled her e-mail back up and opened the most recent mail from the Bent Creek PD. She replied to it and wrote:

*Thanks so much for the help. I was wondering if I could get a few other things as soon as possible. I'd like to get a list of family members related to the McCauleys that live within a fifty-mile radius, along with contact information. If you have the number for Delores Manning's agent, that would be great, too.*

She felt almost lazy requesting the information in such a way. But if they were offering to help so effortlessly, she wanted to use the Bent Creek PD as a resource as much as she could.

With that done, Mackenzie opened up another file…a file that she had managed to tuck away and not obsess over for nearly three weeks now. She opened it up, cycled through the files, and pulled up a single photograph.

It was a business card with her father's name scrawled on the back. On the other side, showed in another photo, was a business name in bold lettering: **Barker Antiques: Old or New Rare Collectibles**.

And that was it. She already knew that no such place existed—not as far as she or the FBI could tell—which made it all the more frustrating. She eyed the card and felt a pull at her heart. She was about two and a half hours away from the place her father had died and maybe three hours away from where the business card in the photo had been found—nearly twenty years after her father's death.

It was not her case...not really. McGrath had given her something of an under-the-table pass at assisting when she could but so far, the case had remained cold. She thought of Kirk Peterson, the detective who had uncovered the new clues that had reopened her father's case. She nearly called him up but realized that it had somehow gotten to be 11:45. And besides that, what would they talk about other than the silence coming from the current and reopened cases?

But she needed to call him. Maybe after this case, when she could give Peterson and the case her full attention. It was about time she got that damned monkey off of her back.

She readied herself for bed, brushing her teeth and changing into a thin pair of sweatpants and a T-shirt. Just before she settled into bed, she checked her phone one last time for any late incoming mails.

She saw that her e-mail request for information from the Bent Creek PD had already been responded to, having come in a mere seventeen minutes after she had sent it. She jotted the information down in her files and made a mental schedule for the following day. She then finally allowed herself to turn off the lights and go to bed.

She did not like ending a day and turning out the lights on unanswered questions. It was an unsettling feeling that she supposed she'd never get used to. But she had adapted long ago, finding a way to sleep a few fitful hours while the answers to her questions lurked in the darkness of night comfortably out of her grasp.

## CHAPTER EIGHT

Mackenzie had just finished getting dressed when someone knocked on the door of her motel room. She checked through the peephole and saw Ellington standing there. He was holding a small cardboard box with two cups of coffee perched on top. She opened the door and let him in, not sure how to feel about him being ready for the day before her. She had always prided herself on her promptness and her tendency to be early. It now looked like she might have some competition in that area.

"Am I interrupting the complicated morning flow of a woman getting ready?" he joked as he set the box and the coffees down on the small table by her already-made bed.

"No, I just finished up," she said, gladly taking the coffee.

Ellington flipped the box open and revealed half a dozen donuts. "Sure, it's a cliché," he said. "But damn…is there anything better than fresh donuts?"

In response, she picked one up and took a bite.

"So what's today look like?" he asked.

"Why are you asking me?"

He shrugged and took up his own donut. "Let's shoot straight, White. I know enough about you to know that you work better when you're in control. That's not to say that you aren't a good backup or partner. But facts are facts. I have no problem with you running things here. I want to see you shine just as much as McGrath. So, I repeat my question: What's today look like?"

"Well, I looked through the missing persons cases over the last ten years last night," Mackenzie answered. "There was only one case that was worth looking into—a car accident during an ice storm where a woman was thrown from the car and her body was never found. Vicki McCauley."

"How long ago was this?" Ellington asked.

"It happened in 2009. I got the information for a single family member within the area and think it might be worth looking into. I also want to give Delores Manning's agent a call. Maybe they know personal details about her life that might help us. The fact that Manning has family so close to the areas where the disappearances are occurring makes me think her personal life might be worth looking into."

"Well then, let's get to it," Ellington said.

Mackenzie checked her phone and saw that it was 7:50. She grinned at him and sipped from her coffee. It was black, which she usually didn't care for, but she wasn't going to complain.

"You're a morning person, huh?" she said.

"It depends on the case. The more answers there are to find, the easier it is for me to roll out of bed."

"Well, seeing as how we have a grand total of *no* answers for this one, I guess you were up very early this morning."

He gave a nod and took a gulp of his coffee as they headed out of her room and to the parking lot. As they got into the car— Ellington in the driver's seat and Mackenzie already pulling up the number for Delores Manning's agent—Mackenzie thought Ellington was on to something. It *was* a bit easier to hit the ground running when there were no answers at their disposal. The sense that there was something to be discovered out there that could lead them to the three missing women made the morning seem a little more promising. And it made her all the more anxious to get to work.

*  *  *

When Mackenzie got Harriett Wheeler on the phone, she knew right away that she had woken the woman up. Wheeler, who had been Delores Manning's agent for the last four years, sounded tired and cranky when she answered the phone on the fourth ring.

"Hello?"

"Hi, Ms. Wheeler. This is Agent Mackenzie White with the FBI. I was wondering if you might be able to answer a few questions for me."

"About Delores, I assume?"

"Yes, about Delores. I apologize for the early call, but as I'm sure you understand, time is of the essence."

"Yes, I get that. I jumped at the phone just now because I was kind of hoping you'd be a policeman or maybe even Delores herself to tell me everything was good now. But I assume she's still missing?"

"Yes. So any new information you can provide is going to help us find her much faster."

"Well, I already spoke to the police."

"I know. My main question concerns people Delores knew. For instance, did you know that her family lived out here in Iowa?"

"I did, but she never really talked about them. I got the feeling that she was sort of ashamed of her family situation."

*That's easy to believe,* Mackenzie thought, recalling the visit to the trailer park yesterday.

"Did anyone else know that she was making this trip?" Mackenzie asked.

"Just the bookstores she was signing at and our PR guys. But they've been here in the office for the last week."

"How long had Delores been out traveling?"

"Four days. She started in Nebraska, then went to Iowa, and then she had a signing scheduled in Chicago. After that, it was back to New York."

"Was anyone traveling with her?"

"No. She loved to drive herself on these trips. This would have been her third trek across most of the country to do these signings. Outside of the actual writing, I think it was her favorite part of the job."

"Are there any enemies you can think of? Maybe even just competition in terms of writing or sales?"

"Not at all," Wheeler said. "Delores really is a sweetheart. If she had any enemies, they stayed quiet and I never knew about them."

With that, Mackenzie's line of questions ran dry. It had gone pretty much as expected. Wheeler knew just enough about Delores to say they had a comfortable working relationship. Outside of that, there was no real connection.

"Well, thank you for your time. And please call me right away if anything comes to mind."

"Of course," Wheeler said. "Thank you."

Mackenzie ended the call and looked out the window. They had already started passing by the forests of Bent Creek, headed to another small town half an hour away.

"Nothing good with the agent?" Ellington asked.

"No," Mackenzie said. "She *did* say that Delores had done three trips across the country for book signings, though. So she was something of a seasoned traveler. I assume that means secondary roads really didn't scare her."

"So no real information to use there," Ellington said.

"Not really," Mackenzie said. "So...next up is the McCauley family member. The only information we have is that it's Vicki McCauley's aunt, but through a blended family situation."

"So you think that's going to be grasping at straws, too?" Ellington asked.

"I guess we'll just have to see."

The car fell into silence and stayed that way for about ten minutes. Mackenzie could feel the beginnings of conversations stirring in the car but they never came to anything. This was fine with her; she and Bryers had never really mastered the art of small talk, either. If Ellington was anything like her (and she was beginning to find that he was in a lot of ways), he was simply running the facts of the case through his head, processing as he drove.

"So do you miss it out here?" he asked her, seemingly out of nowhere.

"Out here?" she asked. "This isn't Nebraska."

He chuckled and said, "I know. But potato, po*tah*toe."

He was right, but she didn't want to admit it. Still, she looked out the window and could safely say that there *were* aspects of the rural landscape that she missed. The winding landscapes, the absolute quiet (especially at night when the crickets came out in little armies to sing their songs), and the feeling that the world went on forever. She missed those things. But in terms of her place in life, she did not miss it at all.

"No, not really," she said, giving the shortened answer.

"It *is* nice in some ways. The lack of buildings and traffic. I almost moved out to Arizona for the very same reason when I was out of college."

"Yeah? Why Arizona?"

"Why not? I always thought the desert pictures I saw from out that way were beautiful. But then DC came calling and I just couldn't turn down the lure of the gun, the badge, and those three iconic letters…*F, B, I*."

She understood what he meant when he said *lure*. That was probably the best way she could describe it. Even when working as a detective in Nebraska, there had been a dream on the other end of some invisible line, calling to her, luring her closer.

And now she was there, walking along the edges of that dream and trying to better understand it. With that thought in her head, she couldn't help but smile. It was a smile that pushed any remaining vestiges of pining for this part of the country out of her heart and dedicating it strictly to DC and the life she was building for herself there.

\*\*\*

Frances Foster lived in a nice-looking Colonial-style house at the end of a short unmarked back road. The town she lived in made

41

Bent Creek look like a booming metropolis. Mackenzie counted only a single stoplight before Ellington turned off of the main stretch of road and onto the back road Frances Foster lived on.

Mackenzie had called ahead, using the cell number she'd been provided with, so Frances was already standing at the front door. She was opening it for them before they even stepped up onto the porch. She looked to be in her early fifties, a feature that seemed both odd and quaint when Mackenzie also noted the Hogwarts shirt she was wearing.

They made a quick round of introductions and then headed inside. Mackenzie again noticed that Ellington was making a point to hang back, letting her have the lead.

"Thanks so much for meeting with us," Mackenzie said as Frances led them through the living room.

"Of course," Frances said. "It's always odd to hear Vicki's name. And there are times when I *do* hear it that I nearly forget that she died under such odd circumstances."

She had led them to a large back room that Mackenzie assumed was a study. A quick glance around told Mackenzie that Frances worked from home. A MacBook sat alongside a large desktop monitor. A tidy stack of papers was to the right of the monitor, resting in front of a well-organized rack of more papers, writing utensils, and a stapler.

Frances took a seat at her rollaway chair behind her desk, swiveling it to face them. Meanwhile, Mackenzie sat down on a small loveseat in the corner while Ellington opted to stand.

"Were you and Vicki close?" Mackenzie asked.

"We weren't best friends or anything," Frances said. "However, when there was a family function of any kind, she and I would always end up finding a quiet corner somewhere to talk."

"So you had shared interests?" she asked.

"I guess you could say that," Frances said. She then plucked at her Hogwarts shirt. "I've always been a big kid. And while Vicki was twenty-five when she died, I kind of viewed her as a kid because she was still into childlike things. Disney movies, Harry Potter, Marvel movies, things like that."

"Can I ask how deeply you knew her? Did she ever talk about work or marital troubles with you?"

"Not especially. I mean, we talked about sex and ex-boyfriends but there was never really anything raunchy. Nothing *too* personal."

"Did she ever talk to you about anyone that she really didn't like?" Mackenzie asked.

"Well, yeah. That would be the ex-boyfriends."

"Sure," Ellington said. "But what about people that she tried to stay away from? Anyone like that?"

Frances moved her mouth, nearly saying something. But she bit back her comment at the last moment as a thoughtful look came over her face. Mackenzie thought she might start crying.

"That was the kind of woman she was, you know?" she said. "No enemies. Not a single person that could say anything against her."

"You're certain of that?" Mackenzie asked. "You specifically mentioned ex-boyfriends."

"Well, Vicki was the kind that boys pined over. I'm sure there were more than a few young men that had their hearts broken. There was one in particular that stands out but I don't think even *he* would be able to do anything overtly illegal. Especially not something like kidnapping...if that's what we are in fact talking about."

"Who's the person you're thinking about?" Mackenzie asked. "You'd be surprised at how the smallest little detail can reap huge advances in a case."

"My goodness...it's been eight years now and I never even considered it. Now, I never knew him personally. But I'd heard of him. I still hear his name from time to time. Stevie Nichols."

"Was that an ex-boyfriend?" Mackenzie asked.

"No. The way she told it, it was a regrettable one-night stand. But he kept calling and dropping by her house even after she and Sam—the man that later became her husband—got serious. Sam had words with him one time and that was the end of it."

"You said you've heard his name a few times since the accident," Mackenzie said. "What do you mean?"

"Well, Stevie is supposedly this big troublemaker. Getting drunk every weekend, starting fights. But he's also supposed to be this small-town Casanova. A real charmer with the ladies despite his reputation. And if he landed Vicki on a one-night stand, I damn near believe it."

Mackenzie turned to Ellington and couldn't help but smile. She was going to ask him if he could call it in to see if they had anything on a man named Stevie Nichols. But he was already pulling out his phone and headed out of the study. For a moment, a chill rode down her back. Bryers had operated in the exact same way.

*Damn, I'm going to miss that man,* she thought.

She suppressed a sigh and turned back to Frances. "Would you happen to know where Stevie Nichols lives?"

43

"Somewhere in Bent Creek. He's a pig farmer from what I understand. So I don't guess it would be too hard to find him."

"Thank you," Mackenzie said. "Is there anything else you can think of that might help?"

"Nothing that I can think of. But then again the Stevie Nichols thing didn't register until just now."

Mackenzie reached into the inner pocket of her coat and handed Frances a business card. "Please call me if you think of anything else."

"Definitely. And…well, if I can ask…why is this coming up again? Why are you interested in that old accident?"

"I can't give details," Mackenzie said. "But it *is* still considered a missing persons case, so any further information you could provide will be helpful."

Sensing that the meeting was over, Frances got to her feet and led them back through the house. Ellington was still on the phone, apparently on hold. Mackenzie thanked Frances one last time before they headed back to their car.

Ellington ended his call as they got into the car. He cranked the engine to life and gave Mackenzie a nod and a smile. "Stevie Nichols lives on a small farm just outside of Bent Creek. He has a history of assault, drunken misconduct, and credit card fraud."

"Sounds like Frances might have been wrong about him being a charmer," Mackenzie said.

"Now that's not fair," Ellington said. "Us charmers come in all shapes and sizes."

"Just drive, would you? I'll call it in to Bateman to see if he wants in on it since it falls within his jurisdiction."

Ellington did just that. His joking had eased the tension that had come with the quiet on the drive to Frances Foster's house but it had not masked the anticipation that sat between them. They had their first lead and things were finally starting to look up. At least that's what Mackenzie told herself when she thought of as many as three women being held somewhere in these rural forests, suffering through God knew what while praying for someone to rescue them.

# CHAPTER NINE

Because they had started so early in the day, it still felt as if they had the whole day ahead of them when they arrived at Stevie Nichols's house. Mackenzie stepped out of the car and was instantly struck by the stench of the place. To call the plot of land in front of them a *farm* was a bit of a stretch. An old house sat at the front of the property. While it wasn't in a major state of disrepair, it did seem to be in very bad need of some maintenance and cleaning. The grass in the yard was mostly dead, fading into darker and darker shades as the back of the property took over. There, a few large pig pens took up most of the rear of the property. A lonely-looking small barn sat off to the left, on its last legs.

"I smell bacon," Ellington said as he got out.

"Shut up," Mackenzie said. "If this is what bacon smells like before it's processed, I may never eat it again."

Behind them, another car pulled into the driveway. It was a Bent Creek PD cruiser, the underside speckled with mud and dirt. Bateman and Roberts got out. Mackenzie noted that Bateman looked very well put together—almost like a completely different man from the one Mackenzie had seen in the conference room the night before.

"Thanks again for the call," Bateman said as the four met up.

"Sure," Mackenzie said. "Like I said, I don't know that it's going to amount to anything, but I thought it was worth checking out."

"But does this really need the resources of four bodies?" Ellington asked.

"Probably not," Bateman said. "But I know Stevie Nichols. He thinks he's a big fish, you know? I don't mind applying some pressure to him."

As they walked toward the house, Mackenzie noticed three men working out back at the pig pens. The others seemed to notice this as well and, as such, they skipped going to the front door and walked around back to the pens. One of the men was working on reinforcing the fence posts to one of the pens. Two others were dishing out slop in the larger pen. Several pigs came running awkwardly to the edge of the pens as the newcomers arrived. Mackenzie had only ever seen pigs at carnivals and petting zoos. These pigs were quite different; they had been fattened up for slaughter. They were also filthy and reeked of mud and waste.

Bateman took the lead, walking to the man who was fixing the fence. "Is Stevie around this morning?" he asked.

Before the man could answer, a voice responded from behind them. "Yeah, I'm here, Sheriff."

They all turned and saw a man coming out of the small barn to the left of the pens. He was carrying a shovel and a five-gallon bucket.

"Stevie, how are you?" Bateman asked.

Stevie Nichols regarded the four people in front of him—two of whom were in police blues, the others in obvious bureau attire. "I was doing just fine until four law enforcement types showed up on my property."

Mackenzie could tell right away that Nichols was going to be a problem. He was the type that would push and push, doing his best to just barely break the boundaries of common sense. Knowing this, she kept herself on her heels, ready to act at any moment. She really didn't like the fact that he had a shovel in his hand.

"Who are these two, anyway?" Nichols asked, gesturing the handle of the shovel toward Mackenzie and Ellington.

"Agents Ellington and White," Ellington said, stepping forward. It was the first time Mackenzie had seen Ellington get almost protective over her, placing himself between her and an obvious troublemaker. She wasn't quite sure how she felt about it.

"FBI?" Nichols asked. "Ah, Christ, what is it you think I've done now?"

"Nothing, hopefully," Bateman asked. "We were hoping you'd be able to answer a few questions for us about Vicki McCauley."

For a moment, Stevie Nichols looked as if he had been slapped. The name had thrown him for a loop; Mackenzie was certain it was not an act. However, she saw something that made her suspicious…something that seemed a little *off*. There was something plastic sticking out of Nichols's back pocket. She wasn't sure, but it looked like two fingers of a pair of plastic gloves—the sort that fast food workers wore. There was something on the tip of one of the fingers…a residue that she could not clearly see.

"What about her?" Nichols asked. "She's been dead for what…eight years now?"

"Assumed dead, yes," Roberts said. "Her body was never found."

"And I'm sure you've heard about the disappearances around Bent Creek lately, right?" Bateman asked.

Mackenzie watched as Nichols took a moment to sort things out. He was choosing his words carefully, clearly caught off guard.

She looked to his back pocket again, that plastic glove still sticking slightly out. She then looked at the man's hands. In her opinion, they were a little too clean for someone who worked on a pig farm.

"Yes, I have," he said finally. "You think...wait, you think those disappearances are somehow connected to Vicki?"

"We hope not," Bateman said. "But we have to consider it even if it is a minuscule chance."

"Well, I don't know what you want from me," Nichols said.

"Well, for starters...a timeline of where you were on the nights these three women went missing."

"Three?" Nichols said. "Way I heard it, there was only two."

Mackenzie caught the tiniest flicker of regret on Bateman's face. He'd let a detail slip about the case—a detail the public was not yet fully aware of. She also noted that Nichols's reaction had seemed genuine. That alone was enough for Mackenzie to be certain that Stevie Nichols was not their guy.

"Can you account for your whereabouts if we give you certain dates and times?" Roberts asked.

"Probably," Nichols said. "But look...I don't have time for this shit. I'm a busy man with things to do."

"That's fine," Bateman said. "Would you allow us to take a look around your property?"

"Absolutely not," Nichols said. "That's a hell of a note...to be subtly accused of kidnapping or killing and then expected to let you nose around my property. So instead of looking around my property, why don't all four of you just go to hell?"

*Damn,* Mackenzie thought. *He's hiding* something. *He didn't take those women, but there's* something *going on here. That plastic glove and his too-clean hands are proof. I really need to get a good look at that glove.*

"Mr. Nichols," she said, "the more cooperative you are, the sooner we can be out of your hair. If you refuse to help us, we'll come right back in a few hours with a warrant to search the place and do whatever we please. Really, it's your choice."

He nodded and said, "Then you go fetch your warrant."

Mackenzie stepped forward, beyond Ellington. She leaned in slightly and then gave an almost dramatic look back to Ellington, Bateman, and Roberts. "Listen, Mr. Nichols...Agent Ellington and I are with the FBI. And dealing with warrants and paperwork is going to not only slow me down, but it's going to irritate the piss out of me. So let's skip the warrant, okay? We can forget about the warrant if you'll agree to making yourself available for answering any questions we have over the next day or so. Is that a fair deal?"

47

"That still ain't fair," Nichols said. "But that's doable."

"Can I have your word on that?" she asked, extending her hand toward him for a shake.

Nichols gave her a strange look, as if she had lost her mind. He raised an eyebrow at her as he took her offered hand. He squeezed it tight as they shook. "Yeah, you have my word."

"Good," Mackenzie said.

She then drew him close and in a single deft move, reached behind him. She plucked the plastic glove out of his back pocket so quickly that she was handing it to Bateman before Nichols was even aware of what had happened. When he *did* realize what was going on, he did his best to push by Mackenzie. She drew his arm up, still holding his hand, and twisted it up and backward.

Nichols let out a yell but did not fight against her. With the position she had his arm in, one wrong move could result in a snapped wrist.

"Sheriff," Mackenzie said, "could you look that glove over and let me know what the residue on the pinky finger might be?"

Amused and a little impressed, Bateman looked the glove over. With the whole glove exposed, Mackenzie saw more of the residue along the underside of it. She also saw that there was more than residue on it; there was some type of powder along the base as well.

Bateman ran his hand along it and sniffed it. He then rubbed the powder between his forefinger and thumb, flicking it into the air when he was done.

"Cocaine," he said.

"Bitch," Nichols said.

Mackenzie released his arm and gave him a little shove toward Ellington. He held him steady while Roberts slapped a set of cuffs on him.

"Now," Bateman said. "Would you like to show me where you're keeping it, or are you going to make me look?"

Nichols said nothing. He did, however, spit on Bateman's shoes.

"Classy," Bateman said. "Now, let's go have a look in your barn."

Ellington gave Nichols a little nudge as they headed toward the barn. He gave Mackenzie a fleeting smile as they went and mouthed the words *"That was awesome"* at her.

*Yeah,* she thought, allowing herself a rare moment to revel in her accomplishments. *Yeah, it kind of was.*

They walked into the barn, Nichols being pushed ahead as he looked down at the floor. It was obvious he was saying nothing. But that didn't matter. What Mackenzie saw within the barn would be enough to send him to prison. There were three work tables, two of which were covered in a crude lab of sorts. Mackenzie had seen similar set-ups before during her training, but never on an actual case. While they had found coke on his glove, it appeared that Nichols was cooking up meth too.

The cocaine, though, was also in abundance within the barn. One of the tables held two boxes, both of which were crammed with individual baggies. Mackenzie picked one up and guessed each one contained about half a pound. There had to be at least a quarter of a million dollars' worth of cocaine in the boxes.

"Good work, White," Bateman said. "This will keep Nichols busy for a while. Well, not busy…just busy with his thoughts in a prison in Des Moines."

A win was a win, sure. But seeing the makeshift meth lab and the boxes of cocaine was just a reminder that she was certain that Stevie Nichols had nothing to do with the disappearances.

And that, in turn, meant the guilty party was still running free.

# CHAPTER TEN

Mackenzie was impressed with the fluidity and promptness of the Bent Creek police department as things escalated with Stevie Nichols. Roberts had cuffed Nichols at 9:55 and he had been booked, processed, and placed into an interrogation room just short of 11:30. As she and Ellington walked into the conference room to meet with Bateman and Roberts, officers who had gone out to the farm continued to either trickle into the station or call with updates.

There was no doubt that Stevie Nichols was innocent of kidnapping Naomi Nyles, Crystal Hall, and Delores Manning. But what he *was* guilty of was the purchase and consequent selling of cocaine within the Bent Creek region and an attempt to sell and distribute crystal meth. A closer inspection of the cocaine by the Bent Creek PD showed that Stevie had been bagging it up and diluting it with cornstarch to make it stretch out.

While Nichols had not yet given up the name of his distributor, he had been more than glad to throw a few of his biggest buyers under the bus. As Mackenzie and Ellington sat down at the conference room table, four Bent Creek officers were heading out to make arrests.

Bateman sat at the head of the conference room table and slid an evidence bag across to Mackenzie. Inside was the glove she had snatched from Nichols's back pocket.

"That was some really good work," he said. "At what point in the conversation did you notice it?"

"About ten seconds in, I guess."

"Well, I know it didn't get us any closer to finding our kidnapper, but you've done the Bent Creek PD a huge favor. We've been looking for the source of the surprisingly large cocaine epidemic within the county and I think it is currently sitting in our interrogation room. So thanks for that."

"You bring up an important point," Mackenzie said, looking up at the dry erase board. It was still filled with the previous night's notes. It seemed to be taunting her, so she looked away. "We are no closer to finding our guy."

"I wonder if it's time to bring in the State PD on this," Ellington said.

"Oh, they've been here already," Bateman said. "But because there were no hot leads, we basically were told 'let us know when it picks up.'"

"It might not hurt to make a request," Mackenzie said. "Because right now, the only productive idea I can come up with is manning officers along the back roads around here."

"That's already in play," Bateman said. "But it seems like the sonofabitch is staking us out somehow."

"How are the officers along the roads staying in touch?" Mackenzie asked.

"Strictly cell phones. No CB...any jackass with a scanner could pick up on the conversations. But you know, if we can get another dozen or so uniforms out on the roads at night, it could help significantly. Maybe the State guys will go for that."

It was a good thought but Mackenzie doubted it would be so easy. She was pretty sure the Iowa State Police would not jive with the idea of sending out manpower to do nothing more than sit along the side of various back roads in a small town.

"Maybe," she said without much enthusiasm. She stood up from the table, feeling stagnant and restless. "Ellington, I'm going to head back to the motel for a second. Are you good here?"

"Yeah, that's fine," he said. He gave her an inquisitive look. "Everything okay?"

"Yeah," she said. "I just need to sit down with the notes, alone."

They shared a quick glance as they left the room, one that she was pretty sure Bateman picked up on. She wasn't too worried about it, as she was beginning to grow convinced that Bateman and Roberts might be involved somehow. It was something about the way he always walked directly behind her, within easy reach of her. He also tended to let his stare linger on her a little too long.

When Mackenzie stepped back outside, it was just after noon. It was one of those clear pleasant days that made her almost want to walk the three blocks to the motel. But she didn't like the idea of being stranded in a place like Bent Creek without a ride. She got into the rental car and headed back to the motel. The case files were there, but, for the moment, they were not on her mind. Suddenly, she needed something else to boost her mind, to get her thinking creatively in the hopes of figuring out how to get one solid lead.

With that, her thoughts turned once again to her father and a twenty-year-old case that still haunted her all the way from Nebraska.

\*\*\*

51

She ordered a pizza for lunch and by the time it was delivered, she had the notes and photos from the new crime scene in Nebraska spread out on the bed along with the archived materials on her father's case. Time and time again, she returned her attention to the business card. It was a strange clue to leave behind and, as far as Mackenzie was concerned, it was a statement being made by the killer.

But because Barker Antiques was apparently not a real place, the killer was not broadcasting a location. He was trying to convey some other message—a message that reached out over two decades. A message no one had yet figured out.

*The same business card almost twenty years later. The same type of killing, the same room of the house, a killer with apparent easy access into the house...*

Maybe it came down to the women in the houses....in her case, it had been her mother. But in terms of the new case, it was the wife of the man that had been killed, asleep on the couch. The set-up was eerily similar in both cases.

Every time she looked at the files, Mackenzie felt like she was missing something. It wasn't something overtly obvious but she felt like there was *something* just under the surface of it all.

*If the killer had access to the houses, they likely knew the families. There was some kind of connection between the killer and the victims or, at the very least, between the killer and the other person that was in the house at the time of the killings.*

She'd considered this before; it was a thought that had almost had her calling her mother on a few occasions to see if she would reveal anything new about the night her father had been killed.

"Hold on," Mackenzie said to herself. She took a seat at the small table by the bed and allowed her mind to shift gears. She pushed aside all thoughts of her father's old case and brought the events of the last two days to the forefront. She ate a slice of pizza, working a few details out in her mind.

*I overlooked the connections angle on the disappearances just because the most recent one was an author. I assumed her fame—no matter how small—eliminated her from being connected to the other victims. But she's from around here, a little over an hour away in Sigourney. What if...*

She picked up her phone and called Ellington. "That was fast," he said. "You miss me already?"

"Can you ask Bateman to get someone working on a connections angle between the victims?" she asked, ignoring his joke.

"You mean finding out if the victims were connected in any way? We went over that at last night's meeting, White. The victims did not know each other."

"I know that," she said. "But maybe each of the victims knows the man that abducted them. Maybe it was a mutual acquaintance. In a town as small as Bent Creek, it has to be at least a good possibility?"

"Yeah, you'd think so," Ellington said, suddenly sounding interested. "I'll get someone on that." There was a pause here and then he asked: "Are you okay?"

"Yes."

She almost told him that she'd been sinking into her father's old case and the more recent case that seemed to be tied to it. She always seemed to grow a little detached when she tried figuring it out. But for now, she figured she'd hold that information close to her chest. The last thing she wanted was for Ellington to offer his services while she wrestled with it.

Mackenzie ended the call and started tidying up the files she had left on the bed. She did her best to clean quickly and get out, but, as usual, she found herself staring at the business card and the bloodstained sheets. It was like the past had come back not only to haunt her but to remind her that even though she had gotten away from Nebraska, her past was not so easy to escape after all.

*Then do something about it,* she thought. *Stop obsessing and dig into it.*

And why not? McGrath had all but given her the green light, and her father's death was the sole reason she had wanted a career in law enforcement.

She pulled up Kirk Peterson's number and nearly called it. She was sure he'd be fine with her checking in. But she also knew that if she called him now and he had even the tiniest bit of news, her mind would be split between these two cases.

*After this case is wrapped up, spend a week or so on nothing but your father's case,* she told herself. *Honestly, you owe it to yourself.*

It was an easy decision to make. She'd discuss it with McGrath when she returned to Quantico. She had to get out from under the weight of her past.

But first, there was the man that had taken Delores Manning and two other women. He was still out there somewhere and the longer he was at large, the slimmer their chances were of catching him. She knew the forecast was calling for snow very soon—maybe as early as tomorrow morning. Once the snow started, it was going to be so much harder to catch him.

Mackenzie peered out of her window and looked at the sky. Right now, it looked blue and non-threatening. But knowing that snow could be on the way, she felt more pressured than ever to get out there and prevent this man from taking another victim.

## CHAPTER ELEVEN

Delores had done her very best to stay alert. She'd only slept once and she was pretty sure that had been for no longer than three hours. Her panic, exhaustion, and fear all mingled to make the last forty-eight hours or so seem like a blur. In that time, she had interacted with her captor just one time. He had slid a plastic bottle of water through one of the rectangular slats in her crate.

She'd figured out it was a crate of some kind shortly after her mind had accepted the fact that she had been captured and was being held prisoner. Acceptance had come hesitantly but once it had settled in, it had cleared the way for something close to logic.

The crate was made of metal. She had felt her way around the small confined box several times and could not quite figure out what it was. Not at first, anyway. She continued to hear the animal sounds she'd heard when she had first come to. Continuing to hear those sounds, Delores started to wonder if she was in some sort of livestock container—maybe the kind that was used to carry cows along the highways. But this container was not quite big enough for a cow. It was a little too spacious to be for a pig, though. Maybe a goat? She didn't know...and trying to figure it out was both menacing and an invitation to madness.

She was also fairly certain that she was being held in a large shed or a small barn. She could still hear that unidentifiable animal noise. Now it reminded her of large rats. On one occasion, she thought she even heard the distant howling of a train horn.

When he had brought her the water, she'd heard the clasps and locks being unlatched on what she guessed was the door to the building as he entered. From time to time, she had also heard her captor speaking in response to the noises the animals made. His voice was usually cheerful and she assumed he was feeding his animals.

His voice had *not* been friendly and cheerful when he had spoken to her. The conversation had been brief and she had not been able to say much, but it had helped her to better gauge her situation. When he had come to her with her water, he had started off with a gruff-sounding "Here."

He'd then slid the water in to her and added: "If you keep your mouth shut, I'll bring you some food later."

"Please," she'd responded. "If you let me out, I won't—"

"Now that's not keeping your mouth shut, is it? Unless you want to starve in there, you'll keep your fucking mouth shut. You do not speak unless I ask you to and that starts right now."

And that had been it. Delores assumed her situation could be much worse. He could be abusing her, raping her, or killing her. She knew full well that those things could *eventually* happen to her, but for now she was alive and unharmed.

He'd given her the water sometime late last night. It was impossible to tell time in the container but she thought it was now sometime either late in the morning of her second day or early in the afternoon. When he had brought it to her, she'd seen her first real glimpse of him through the slats in the container. He was a big bastard, his shoulders wider than any she had ever seen. He looked to be in his mid-to-late forties and had a scruffy grayish beard.

She had memorized his face, wondering if it might do her some good if she ever got out of this hell.

Her stomach was rumbling with hunger and she had to take a piss. She thought about going in the container; she'd been holding it for about six hours now, and the half of the bottle of water she had chugged down had certainly not helped. But urinating in her own prison would be too much like defeat. And until she felt the last breath escaping her body, she did not plan on giving up.

Of course, she had no idea how she would escape. She thought about screaming for help. Even if the screams attracted only her captor, he'd likely open the container and assault her to shut her up. That might be her only chance to escape. But she knew how big he was and wondered if any attempt at escape would only be an invitation for disaster.

She figured the worst-case scenario was that he'd come for her at some point. He had kidnapped her for a reason—surely not to just keep her penned up. And while she did not like to think of what those reasons might be, the thought of being able to stretch her legs and see daylight was a sweet relief to her heart. It was a small glimmer of hope that was drowned out by the dark confined space of the container.

*I'm going to end up pissing in this container,* she thought. *And then I'll be trapped in here with the smell of my own piss, getting stronger and stronger every hour...*

That sad thought was interrupted by the creaking of the barn door. Delores instinctively pushed herself against the back of the container. A million thoughts went racing through her head...visions of escape, visions of being half-beaten to death.

56

She heard his footsteps outside of the container. He shuffled over, blocking the dusty sunlight from spilling in through the slats. She said nothing, just peered through the square of darkness to his shirt, blocking out the light. It was a denim button-up. A pen stuck out of the top of the left breast pocket.

"You okay in there?" he asked.

The question took her by surprise and she wondered if she heard him right. She opened her mouth to respond but apparently not quickly enough. He banged on the side of the container, creating a hollow thrumming noise that vibrated in her bones.

"*Hey!*" he said, nearly shouting.

"Yes. I'm here."

He shuffled a bit more and then started to place something along the rectangular slits in the container. The first item was a granola bar. It slid through with no problem and fell to the floor of the container. He then placed a crinkled McDonald's bag up to one of the slits. It had been folded over and balled up and he had to push hard against it to get it to fall through the hole. When it hit, the smell of something greasy and utterly delicious filled the container.

"Food," he said. "You need more water?"

"No," she said. "But, please…I have to use the bathroom."

"Then do it in there," came the answer.

"I can't do that," she said.

"It'll be fine. You won't be in there much longer."

It was a terrifying comment that sent her crawling to the front of the container. "Please. Don't make me humiliate myself like that. Please let me out to use the bathroom—"

"No, and don't ask ag—"

"I'll do anything you want. Anything. Please…just let me out."

"Anything," the man said, considering the word. While he thought it over, she stared at that denim shirt and pictured the face she'd seen last night to go with it. She thought it might be easier to not know what he looked like; it would be much easier to project the face of a monster.

"If I open this container and you try anything, I'll kill you," he said after about twenty seconds. "I'll give you one minute to squat in the corner and do your business. But there's a price. When you're done, you drop your pants all the way and then you and I are going into one of the pens in here. You'll put both hands on the gate so I can see them and then I'm going to take you from behind. You fight, I'll make it harder than it has to be. I'll get real violent and then I'll hurt you afterwards. Do you understand?"

57

He walked through the steps as if it were something he did all the time. *Take you from behind* was an especially strange way of putting things. She knew what he meant but something about his phrasing made it more sinister in a strange way.

She sensed an opportunity coming and responded before she could let her fear drown out her bravery. "Yes," she said, already thinking of the potential rape.

Her captor hesitated for only a moment and then Delores heard the jingling of keys. She heard a slight clanging as he inserted a key into the lock on the outside of the container.

"Get back against the far wall," he instructed her.

She did as he asked. When she crept backward, a desperate plan etched itself out in her mind and although it seemed almost ridiculous, she knew that this might be her only chance. If she failed, she'd be beaten, raped, and maybe killed. And if she chickened out and did nothing, she'd have to endure the embarrassment of this man watching her urinate and then raping her.

Slowly, the doorway to the container opened. Dusty light spilled in. She squinted her eyes from it and then she saw him peering down at her, having to duck down to look inside.

There was a sick sort of smile on his face. "C'mon," he said.

She did, walking on trembling legs. He offered a hand for support and she realized just how huge his hands were. From outside of the container, he looked even larger than he had when she had viewed him from inside. He was massive.

"This way," he said, placing a hand on her shoulder and leading her to the far corner of the barn.

She did her best not to seem too obvious as she looked around. What she did manage to see, though, was another container like the one she was in. It was empty, the door standing wide open. She also saw a workbench with glass vases and spray paint sitting on it.

"There you go," he said, pointing to the corner.

"Can I at least get some privacy?" she asked.

"No. I'm not turning my back on you. You think I'm stupid?"

A flare of anger rose up in her and it was the deciding factor in going through with her plan. It terrified her but she knew she had to do it.

Embarrassed, she unbuttoned her pants, pulled them down along with her panties, and squatted in front of him. She looked to the ground as she went. The relief was immense but she had never felt more humiliated in her life.

When she was done, he provided nothing for her to wipe with. She pulled her pants back up and the moment they were at her waist, he was there. He took her by the arm and led her to the other side of the barn where there were two old horse stalls.

"That one," he said, pointing to the closest one. "Put your hands on the gate."

She was shaking from head to toe now. But she obeyed because her plan required it. She turned her back to him and the moment her hands were on the gate, his massive hands gripped the waist of her jeans and pulled them down.

"As long as you don't scream," he said, "I'll keep it real gentle."

She could not see him. She only saw the wall of the horse pen in front of her. She could hear his zipper as he undid his pants and then she felt his hand on her back, on her buttocks. He stepped forward and just as she felt him angling to thrust inside of her, she reached back between her legs and grabbed the first thing her fingers found.

Her fingernails dug into his testicles. She gripped them tight, digging her nails in and twisting. He howled in pain, so loud it was ear-piercing.

She turned from the gate, still squeezing harder than ever. She gave one final crushing flex of her fist and then went running. He lunged for her as she did but he went to the ground with his pants around his ankles. Delores managed to get hers up rather easily and ran straight for the door as he howled behind her.

She must have gotten him good; there was blood on her fingers and skin under her nails. But she had no time to enjoy that. She needed to focus on escaping. She nearly fell to the ground but managed to catch her balance. Her captor reached out for her and his grasping hand missed her by less than six inches. He was in clear and visible pain and it took everything within her not to deliver a kick, another punch, *something…*

Delores went through the barn door and stepped outside. The moment she was in open space, she started screaming. She realized almost right away, though, that her screams might be useless. She was in a large backyard that was surrounded by nothing but forest. Another barn sat to her right.

She started for the house, still screaming, but then stopped. In the midst of her screams, she heard something else.

Another voice. Another scream. And it wasn't the man behind her, who was now coming through the barn doors, either. It was a woman…and she sounded terrified.

59

Delores badly wanted to investigate but she knew that she was already on borrowed time. *I'll make it out of here and send the cops,* she thought. *They can find the other woman and bust this creep.*

But she knew she had to check. She ran for the other barn and found it locked. She banged on the door. "Is someone there?" Delores asked.

"Oh my God! Yes!"

The reply was heartbreaking. Even more so because Delores could not get to the woman. "I can't get in right now, but I'll send the police," she said. "Just hold on!"

Delores nearly took off straight ahead, toward the house, but she saw the dirt driveway and wasn't sure she could outrun the man on such a flat stretch. Very far back in the data banks of her memory, she recalled doing research for a book where she'd spoken with a survival expert who had suggested escaping through a forest was much easier than escaping through open plains. And while there were no plains ahead of her, there *were* forests on all sides.

She ran to her left, where the forest was no more than thirty feet away. As she passed the tree line, she dared another look over her shoulder. The man in the denim shirt came after her, still hobbling but coming much faster.

Delores ran into the trees, running blindly through a forest she was unfamiliar with. Already, she had been slapped in the face by a stray branch, causing a thin trail of blood to run down her cheek.

She was done with looking over her shoulder. She knew he was back there and that was enough for her. She had to keep moving, had to trust that these woods would eventually come to an end and deliver her to a road.

She dodged trees and sidestepped stumps but she never stopped moving. She ran in what she thought was a straight line. She could faintly hear the man tearing through the forest behind her but it was drowned out by her own labored breathing and the occasional desperate cry that rose up out of her throat.

And then there was another sound. It was a dreamlike sound because it made no sense, but it was most definitely there. And it was coming from directly ahead of her.

It was the rhythmic churning of some large engine. There was an underlying wind-like sound to it that at first made no sense.

*A train,* she thought then.

And by God, it sounded close.

This pushed her even harder. Behind her, she could hear her captor let out a curse and a strangled *"NO!"*

Apparently, he had heard the train, too. Delores somehow found yet another gear. Her hamstrings were begging for mercy and her lungs felt like dancing flames, but she pushed on. The sound of the train grew louder and she could see thin breaks in the trees revealing slivers of the afternoon sky up ahead.

She didn't know how long she had been running...five minutes maybe but surely no more than ten. Still, it felt like she had run a marathon. Her heart was hammering hard in her chest and she was sweating badly. Still not daring to look back, Delores broke through the tree line ahead of her, the strips of blue she had seen through the trees now a wide open expanse of sky.

And there, twenty yards in front of her, were the train tracks. The train blared by, shaking the ground. She watched the cars roll by, jostling on the tracks and blasting warm air by her. It was then that she chanced a look back over her shoulder. She saw the man in the denim shirt coming through the trees. The look of maniacal hatred on his face was terrifying...enough to get Delores running for the train.

*And just what in the hell do you think you're going to do?* she asked herself.

She knew what she was going to *try.* And if it didn't work, the worst that might happen was that she'd die. And if she died, she wouldn't have to concern herself with what this pervert had in store for her.

"Oh my God, oh my God," Delores started to chant.

She ran toward the train. With each sprint ahead, she could feel its vibrations in her feet. They traveled up to her stomach and even seemed to cause her eyes to tremble. She watched as one car passed, then another. Her eyes relayed the information to her brain and even though her muscles seemed to want no part of this insane plan, she continued running forward.

She took in the racing shapes of the train cars, knowing her chances were slim, knowing that basic physics was working against her and that she—

She saw the thin rails of handholds on the side of one of the cars and before she could talk herself out of it, she jumped.

Her right hand found the rung of the makeshift ladder that scaled the side of the car. Her body followed her extended arm and slammed into the lower edge of the car. Her grip nearly released from the impact but her left hand then scrambled and found purchase on the rung. By the time she realized she was somehow holding on, she also felt the tug of gravity at her legs.

61

She was dangling from the train car, her legs whipping like paper in the breeze. Delores cried out and reached up to the next rung. She pulled herself upward, the shaking from the car and the tracks like some invisible hands pushing against her. With a scream of determination, she managed to reach to another rung and finally set her feet on the lower-most rung.

*Now what?*

She had no idea. She looked backward and could see the man that had been chasing after her. He was a shrinking speck in the distance. She then trained her eyes on the edge of the car. It was a faded red color, complete with a sliding door, the latch of which was about three feet away from her left arm. From what she could tell, the latch was loose; it had not been secured.

She could feel adrenaline speeding through her body, could even taste something like copper in the back of her throat as her body was soaked with it. She crept to the farthest edge of the rungs of the thin ladder and then stretched her left hand out.

Just before her fingers touched it, the door slid open. It happened so suddenly that Delores shouted out in surprise. A man looked out to her and for a sickening moment, she was sure it was him—the man in the denim shirt that had kept her in the container. But a simple blink of the eyes showed her a haggard man, looking to be in his sixties. His white beard was filthy and his eyes were wide and confused.

"What the effing *hell*?" the man said. "Lady, are you *nuts*?"

She supposed it was a vagrant, a drifter who hopped rail cars to get from place to place. Whatever he was, he was her savior in that moment. He reached out to her, offering his hand, and she took it.

"Can you do this?" the man asked.

Delores nodded, but she was crying. She fumbled for the man's hand, took it, and gave it a hard squeeze which she did not release. The man gave her a nod and pulled. Delores let go of the rung, screaming. She felt herself falling down but also straight across. The old man looked very weak and she feared that she'd only pull him out of the car with her, sending them both to their deaths to the embankment below the tracks.

What she felt instead was something hard slamming into her stomach and then the feel of something solid and steady beneath her. The old man had managed to pull her into the car. Her feet were still dangling out. She pulled them in quickly, sobbing and gasping for breath.

"Thank you," she managed to wheeze to him.

He was kneeling by her, looking her over. He smelled atrocious but in that moment, he was the most glorious man on the face of the planet as far as Delores was concerned.

"What the hell were you doing out there?" he asked her.

She tried talking but it all came out in sobs. The few words she did manage to get out, though, told most of the story. *"A man...kidnapped me...two days...escaped..."*

"My God," the old man said.

Had she not been in a tremendous amount of pain, her eyes glazed with tears and her heart still pumping wildly, she might have noticed the peculiar look in the man's eye. She might also have noticed that he was unbuttoning his filthy pants.

"Well then," the man said, "that makes me feel *real* bad about what I'm going to do."

She barely had time to register the words before the man's hands were in her hair. She gasped in surprise and pain as he lifted her head up off the floor. When he slammed it back down, the noise it made seemed amplified inside of her own head. The man then did it two more times. On the third strike, Delores slipped away, feeling something sharper than sleep coming toward her as the almost-gentle trembling of the train car lured her further down.

## CHAPTER TWELVE

One of the things that drove Mackenzie absolutely nuts was chasing down a lead and knowing almost right away that it would produce nothing. The only reason she was not feeling totally defeated as she and Ellington drove down a side street in Bent Creek was because she also knew that sometimes even the weakest lead could produce some sort of fruit.

After four hours of phone calls, checking records, cross referencing, and searching the Bent Creek archives from the past twenty years or so, Mackenzie, Ellington, and a team of four Bent Creek officers had only come up with one potential lead—one single person that connected the three victims. And it was a tenuous connection at best.

"You look depressed," Ellington pointed out as he slowly drove down the side street in search of a particular house.

"No...just not a fan of hunting leads that likely won't pan out."

"Oh, I feel you there," Ellington said. "But an instructor of mine at the bureau once had a pretty great analogy about thoroughly investigating every single lead, no matter how hopeless. He said to imagine walking along a river after a rain and kicking over every rock you get to. There's going to be *something* under every rock: worms, bugs, debris. Every rock will reveal something different than the last, therefore they are *all* worth looking under."

"Fitting," she said. "But I'd rather not think of potential leads as rocks to kick."

Ellington parked the car, having finally found the house in question, and shrugged. "Eh, whatever works for you, I guess."

They got out of the car and looked at the house in front of them. It belonged to the grandmother of Naomi Nyles, eighty-one-year-old Mildred Cole. When they had called from the station, the old lady had seemed a little too excited to be receiving company, even if it was in the form of FBI agents coming to ask about the disappearance of her granddaughter. She'd even given them the go-ahead to knock and then come in because, as she put it, her "damned hip keeps flaring up and I never know when it's going to lock up, so I just stay in my chair all the time."

Following the old woman's directions, Mackenzie and Ellington walked inside after knocking. "Hello, Ms. Cole?" Mackenzie said as they stepped into a small foyer.

"Yeah, in here," came an old cheerful voice from the right of the foyer.

64

They walked into the living room and found Mildred Cole sitting in a large recliner. A glass of iced tea sat on an end table beside her and the television was loud and blaring. Currently, she was watching a home renovation show.

"Thanks for agreeing to meet with us," Ellington said.

"Sure, sure," Mildred said. "Ain't like I got much else to do, now, you know?"

"Well, we'll try to make it quick," Mackenzie said, having to nearly shout to be heard over the television. Mildred eventually picked up on this and muted the TV with a remote that she pulled out of one of the recliner's many folds.

"I guess they still haven't found Naomi, have they?" Mildred asked.

"No, ma'am," Ellington said.

"But we're hoping to uncover anything about the lives of the missing women that we can," Mackenzie added. "That includes looking for even the smallest connection. And as we were looking through the backgrounds of these three missing women, we found one solid connection. And that was *you*. And since you happen to be the grandmother of one of the missing, it seemed like an obvious lead for us."

"I saw the news about the third lady today on TV," Mildred said. "Delores Manning. A sweetheart if I ever knew one."

"Speaking of which," Mackenzie said, "we uncovered the fact that you once babysat Delores. Do you recall how long you watched her?"

"Oh, I don't remember exactly," Mildred said. "Her mother was never really in the picture, you know. Sometimes Delores was here until eight or nine at night before her mom would pick her up—drunk off her ass, I might add. I guess Delores was about thirteen or so when she stopped coming here."

"And other than her mother, was there any drama with Delores?"

"None that I remember. She was always a good kid, writing in her notebooks. She always knew she wanted to be a writer."

"Now, for Crystal Hall," Ellington said. "Our research shows that you once worked for her father at the slaughterhouse in town. Is that right?"

"Oh yes. And that poor girl would be there sometimes. She'd go to her father's office after school and do her homework. Her dad was always busy…a good man but busy as hell, you know the type. Her mother passed when she was nine and the family never recovered. So I'd help Crystal with her homework as well as I

65

could. But when it got to algebra and nonsense like that, I wasn't any help. She was a sweet kid. I think when she got older, though, she became a little…well…she liked the boys. I'll leave it at that."

"You mean she was promiscuous?" Mackenzie asked.

"That's putting it mildly. The first time she was caught was behind a convenience store at the age of fourteen, I think. The man she was…well, *servicing* was nineteen. The gossip mill says that on two occasions, her father hunted her down and found her out in the woods with boys. Found her right in the act one time."

"How long ago was that?" Mackenzie asked.

"Oh, I'm not too sure. Ten years? Maybe twelve?"

"Were you still talking to her after that?" Ellington pried.

"No. And I get it. These little girls that knew me when they were younger don't have much need for an old woman in their lives, you know? I haven't spoken to any of them in at least ten years. Just a nod here and there on the street when I was still able to get out. But Delores did send me a copy of her first book with a thank-you note. Sweet girl…"

"So, you have no idea what might link them together?" Mackenzie asked. "Can you think of any reason why someone might have targeted them?"

The old woman frowned and sipped from her iced tea. "No. People are just mean as hell these days, ain't they? I mean, would someone even need a reason or connection other than they're just mean?"

This question was met with silence. Mackenzie looked around the living room, taking in the photos of family members, the family Bible on the coffee table, and old books scattered here and there on even older shelves and a rickety book case.

"Well, thank you again for your time," Ellington said.

"Oh, you going already?" Mildred asked. "At least stay for a glass of tea. Keep an old lady company for five minutes, won't you?"

Mackenzie opened her mouth to politely decline, but Ellington beat her to it. "You know, I think we can do that," he said, giving Mackenzie a quick grin. "You just tell me where it is and I'll pour it. No need in you getting up."

Mildred cackled and made a huge show of slowly getting out of the recliner. "Oh, I ain't given up quite that bad just yet."

As she made her way out of the living room and toward the hallway beyond, she was still chuckling. Mackenzie smiled at Ellington, finding his decision to stay both sweet and fascinating. The man was apparently full of surprises.

"It'll be okay," he said quietly. "Besides, it's sweet tea. And the older the old lady, the sweeter the tea. And I can't pass up a glass of sweet tea."

Mackenzie had no idea how to respond, so she stayed quiet. She looked around the living room, trying to imagine a younger Delores Manning sprawled on the floor with a notebook and a pen. She saw this ghost image in front of her until she was interrupted by the clinking of ice in two glasses of sweet tea coming toward them from the hallway.

Even as they sat there for another five minutes with Mildred, Mackenzie was already thinking about the stories the old woman had told them and how she might use them to hunt down another lead.

*Crystal Hall's father,* she thought. *He's certainly not our guy but with a daughter with a reputation like hers, he's sure to have information on the lowlife men in this town. It's maybe the best lead we have so far.*

With that little nugget in mind, it was a little easier for her to sit still and enjoy the tea almost as much as Ellington did.

\*\*\*

Dusk was falling as they headed out to their car. As Ellington got in behind the wheel, he looked over to Mackenzie and grinned. "So, who's going to make the call?"

"What call?" she asked.

"To Crystal Hall's father. That's the next step, right?"

It was beyond eerie how quickly he had been able to almost sync himself to her level. She *had* been thinking that it would be a good bet to speak with Crystal Hall's father while they'd been sipping sweet tea. Maybe they could get a few names from him—of the men Crystal had been involved with. It was yet another long shot, but it was better than no shot at all.

"I'll make the call to Bateman," she said.

"Sounds good. So tell me...sweet tea aside, is it safe to say that the visit to Mildred Cole's house was mostly a bust?"

"No, I wouldn't say that," Mackenzie said. "We got some insights into these women. We know more about them now. Any small details could come in handy later down the road. And we now have the very vague and probably dead-end idea to speak with Crystal Hall's father. As you might put it, it was a rock that needed kicking over."

"You'll be thinking like me in no time," Ellington said.

"That's terrifying," she said, scrolling to Bateman's number.

Prompt as always, Bateman answered just after the first ring. "Hey, Agent White. Anything new?"

"Not yet," she said. "But look, we just spoke to Mildred Cole. I think it might be worth speaking to Crystal Hall's father. Is he still around the Bent Creek area?"

"Oh yeah. And you know…it's five fifty-seven right now. I can almost guarantee he'll be easy to find. Just make a stop by Bumper's Bar between now and about nine o' clock."

"Even now, less than ten days after his daughter being taken?"

"Yes, even now. I think he's under the impression that she just moved away. It's a weird family. Really screwed-up dynamic there. I'll shoot you over a recent mugshot from about five months ago when we brought him in on a drunk and disorderly."

"Thanks," Mackenzie said. "We'll keep you posted."

She ended the call and looked to Ellington. "Feel like hitting up a bar?"

"Always."

She pulled up the directions for Bumper's Bar and navigated the way. She got an e-mail from Bateman containing the picture of Crystal Hall's father. The information in the placard listed him as Donald M. Hall, age fifty-one. She then looked out to the streets. The night was pressing down, the first stars beginning to show and the threat of snow still looming.

All Mackenzie could think of was how this was just an opportunity for their man to strike.

## CHAPTER THIRTEEN

Mackenzie had never liked country music and whenever she walked into a bar and it was the first thing she heard, she cringed inside. It was no different when she and Ellington walked into Bumper's Bar. Bumper's was quite a bit nicer than the bar beside the Motel 6 that she and Ellington had visited. There was no real crowd to speak of, just a handful of men sitting at the bar and a loud table of twenty-somethings in the far corner working on a pitcher.

Mackenzie spotted Donald Hall right away, sitting at the farthest edge of the bar. Another man sat beside him but they were not speaking. Donald Hall was staring blankly at the small television behind the bar currently set on mute and showing two sports broadcasters on ESPN. She once again watched Ellington assume the role of reluctant protector as he took the lead while they walked across the bar. Mackenzie noticed two men at the bar checking her out. Their eyes on her were like bugs on her skin. She was glad Ellington was there with her. If not, some creep might say something to her and she'd end up throwing a punch or two.

They approached Donald Hall, keeping their distance a bit but sidling up to the bar. "Mr. Hall?" Mackenzie asked.

He turned toward them and she could see that there was already a slight drunken haze to his eyes. He had the look and demeanor of a seasoned drinker. Mackenzie figured him as the type that got hammered at least twice a week and just mildly drunk the other five nights. Being that his daughter was just reported missing, she expected the ratio was a bit different now—even if he *did* think Crystal had simply left town without bothering to tell anyone.

"Who are you?" he asked.

"We're with the FBI," Mackenzie said. "I'm Agent White, this is Agent Ellington. We were hoping to speak with you about what happened to your daughter."

"What do you want to know?" he asked. He seemed more annoyed than anything. If he felt anything about his daughter being MIA, he was hiding it incredibly well.

"Maybe we could speak somewhere more private?" Mackenzie suggested.

"No, I'm good here. Besides…there's nothing to tell. Everyone in town knows the kind of girl Crystal was. Especially the fucking men."

"Could you elaborate on that?" she asked.

69

Donald gulped from his beer and looked to Mackenzie as if she were stupid. "Well, let's see...she was caught by myself and the police four different times between the ages of fourteen and seventeen banging dudes in cars and even blowing one guy behind a store. She left home at seventeen to live with some guy that got her pregnant and bailed after shucking out the money for an abortion. She moved to Des Moines to escape her problems but had to travel out this way to visit the farms for her job. Last year she was caught sleeping with one of the farmers. His wife found out and left him. So yeah...my little Crystal is well known around here."

"And I've been told by Sheriff Bateman that you don't think she was abducted."

"Nope. She's been getting reprimanded by her supervisors out at Wrangler Beef for the way she behaves. She was never cut out for a job...well, not a real job, anyway. Did Bateman tell you that when she got busted at the age of sixteen, there was money involved? One hundred bucks so some thirty-year-old could spend an hour in a back seat with her. She was never responsible. I think she ditched her car, seeing that someone else had gone missing— this Naomi Nyles girl—and ran away from her responsibilities. God knows where she is right now and what she's doing."

"And you have no interest in finding out?"

Donald Hall turned away from her and stared back to the TV. "No. Now...are we done here?"

"One more question, if you don't mind," Mackenzie said. "This farmer that lost his wife because of the affair. Who was it?"

"It don't matter. His wife left and he moved to Texas."

"And what about some of these other men Crystal has been caught with in her past?" Ellington asked. "Do any of them jump out to you as being suspicious or just made for trouble?"

Donald thought about this for a second and bit down on a thin smile. "You know," he finally said, "actually, yeah. The jackass that paid for her. His name is Mitch Young."

"Does he live around here?"

"Yeah. He holes up in a rundown trailer out in the woods off of State Route 14."

Mackenzie and Ellington shared a look and a single word seemed to pass between them.

*Bingo.*

\*\*\*

After getting directions from Bateman, Ellington headed back out to State Route 14. Seeing the road in the darkness of the early hours of night seemed foreboding. It was literally like revisiting the scene of the crime. As they made their way to the address, they passed one of the dirt tracks that had been cabled off—the dirt roads that had caught Mackenzie's attention when they had first come down this road yesterday.

"Coincidence?" Ellington said.

"Could be," Mackenzie said. "This part of the state is filled with back roads. Still, if this turns out to be promising, Bateman and three others are on standby."

Ellington headed another half a mile down the road and turned left onto another dirt road. This one was speckled with gravel but looked in rough shape. When he turned onto it, Mackenzie realized that it was supposed to be a driveway. Being that it was on the same side of the road as both of the blocked dirt tracks she had spotted yesterday, it raised a red flag in her head.

The driveway to Mitch Young's place was almost ridiculously long. Mackenzie estimated that they had driven nearly a quarter of a mile before she spotted the trailer up ahead of them. It looked like the trailer was on its last legs. Two cinderblock steps led to the front door. The thing looked like it was about to fall apart—a strong wind might do the trick. Two beat up trucks and a small van sat in a dusty driveway. It all looked shady in the darkness and even more so when the headlights of their car spilled over all of it.

"Holy shit," Ellington said. "White, do you see that?"

She looked beyond the vehicles and the dilapidated trailer in front of them. To the right of the trailer in an overgrown strip of land she assumed was the backyard were two storage containers. They were about three feet tall and maybe four or five feet wide.

"Something doesn't feel right about this," Ellington said.

"Agreed," she said. "I'm going to get Bateman on the phone." She did so and she did it quickly. When he answered, she skipped the pleasantries and simply said: "We need you out here quickly. Nothing bad yet but warning signs all over the place."

She ended the call before Bateman had a chance to respond. She and Ellington then shared a look and stepped out of the car. Right away, they could hear loud yet muffled music coming from the trailer. A guitar solo was trickling into the night, along with a bass line Mackenzie recognized.

From the other side of the car, Ellington made a slight sound of disgust. "Ugh. Skynyrd. This guy *has* to be bad news."

She appreciated the attempt at humor—and was beginning to understand that this was how Ellington handled stress—but still felt the need to keep her hand by her sidearm. Right now, this was nothing more than a typical visit for information and there was no *real* reason to suspect danger other than the man's past charges of lewd conduct with a minor.

They skipped the front door for the time being, heading directly for the backyard. Mackenzie approached the first container and used the flashlight on her phone to peer inside. It was rusted out, complete with a shattered hole in the back. It looked to be made out of some sort of industrial plastic. The second one was in identical shape—neglected and worn down. If it had been used to hold people any time lately, they wouldn't have had much difficulty escaping.

They walked quietly back to the front of the house as Ellington looked around in disgust while approaching the cinderblock steps.

There was only room for one of them on the makeshift stairs. When Mackenzie stepped up onto them, they wobbled a bit. When she knocked on the door, she could feel how flimsy it was.

From inside, she heard someone utter a quick *"Shit..."*

She then heard a slight commotion as things were moved around inside. She knocked again, this time following it up by saying, "This is Agent Mackenzie White with the FBI. I hear you inside, Mr. Young, and would appreciate it if you'd answer the door."

The commotion stopped for a moment and after a silence of five seconds or so, she got a response. "Hold on a second."

Mackenzie looked down at Ellington and saw that his right hand was also hovering over his sidearm. She was glad to know she wasn't the only one who felt a sense of doom in the air. A thought then occurred to her...a dangerous one, maybe, but strategic.

She gave Ellington a *move away* gesture as she whispered to him. "Don't let him know there are two of us. If there's anything shady, he's more likely to show his hand if there's just one of us."

He tilted his head and frowned, clearly not a fan of the idea. But at the last moment, be backed away into the shadows along the side of the trailer.

The moment he was concealed in the darkness, the flimsy front door opened. An overweight man in a tattered white T-shirt and ripped blue jeans stared out at her. He looked almost amused to see her standing there.

"What can I do for you?" he asked.

He was being intentionally smug. He was also doing his very best to block the doorway so she could not see inside.

"I'm investigating a string of disappearances in the area," she said. "One of the missing women is Crystal Hall. My investigation brought your name up."

"Honey, Crystal Hall is a name that's going to come up when you talk with damn near any man in town."

"Maybe," Mackenzie said. "But not all of them paid one hundred dollars to have sex with a minor in the back of a car."

"That was almost ten years ago," Young said. "I paid my dues for that."

"I understand that. I was just hoping you could answer some questions for me."

"I don't think I'd be much help."

"Let me be the judge of that."

"Look, sweetie…I'm sorry Crystal is missing but I'm not the man you need to be talking to. After that night we got busted, I only saw her one other time. And we didn't do much talking."

"Did you pay her then, too?"

"No."

"Mr. Young, would you mind telling me what you use the containers in your backyard for?"

"Nothing, really. Just keeping stuff in."

"Would you mind if I took a look in them?" she asked.

"You got a warrant?"

"No."

"Then no. You can't look around my shit because some slut is missing and I happened to have sampled the goods. So why don't you get on up the road, sweetie, and—"

"Please stop that. Call me *honey* or *sweetie* one more time and I will aggressively get a warrant and search every inch of this place."

"On what grounds?"

"Suspicion. It took you a while to get to the door. What were you moving around inside?"

"None of your business. I was cleaning. Now get the fuck off of my property."

Mackenzie was working on a strong hunch—a hunch that told her there was certainly something inside the trailer. She stepped up on the top cinderblock and stood toe to toe with him. "Mr. Young, I'm going to have to insist that you let me come inside."

"And if I don't?"

73

"Then you go from having just *me* taking a look around to about three other agents along with local PD in a few hours with a warrant. Your call."

"Well, I think I—"

He moved quickly then—or what passed for quickly for him—and went to his side. He managed to get his hand on the butt of a gun that was resting there but he was never able to draw it.

Mackenzie delivered an open-palmed strike to his chest. As he stumbled backward, she shoved her arm beneath his right armpit and lifted him up and over. She dropped him to the ground in a nearly perfect hip toss. When he hit the ground he let out a whooping cough as the gun he had been reaching for clattered to the ground.

In one graceful stride, Mackenzie jumped down from the cinderblock steps and kicked the gun away. She then drew her own gun and pointed it at him. "Stay on the ground and place your hands over your head, interlocked."

He started to get up from the ground, not seeing Ellington moving in to his left. Ellington also drew his gun and held it steady, inches from Young's back. "Do what the lady says."

Slowly, Young placed his hands above his head and laced his fingers together. He was still hitching for breath from being dropped from the doorway, about three feet from the ground.

"Trying to draw a gun on an FBI agent," Ellington said. "What could you be hiding that's so important?"

"Fuck both of you," Young said.

"That's not very nice," Ellington said. "Agent White, if you're okay here, maybe I'll go take a look inside really quick?"

"Go ahead," she said.

Moving quickly, Ellington went into the trailer. Within ten seconds, Mackenzie could hear an exaggerated whistling noise from Ellington. He was back out thirty seconds later, carrying a few glass vials and several small bags of what looked like either small crystals or large grains of sea salt.

"Nice cheap little meth lab you have in there," Ellington said.

Mackenzie realized that this was the second drug bust they had inadvertently made in less than twenty-four hours. *What are the chances?* she thought.

With her gun still trained on Mitch Young, she started to hear the sounds of sirens in the distance as Bateman and his men raced to the scene. In the isolated spaces within the trees off of State Route 14, it sounded almost like ghosts approaching.

The positive takeaway was that they had captured another of Bent Creek's main drug sources. The negative, of course, was that the containers out back were empty. Mitch Young was not their guy.

She took a moment to look at the surrounding trees, wondering just how deep those woods went and how easy it might be for someone to hide there, watching traffic at night and waiting to strike one more time.

## CHAPTER FOURTEEN

Outside of chain restaurants, Bent Creek had only two other options. Two hours after leaving Mitch Young's residence, Mackenzie and Ellington found themselves in one of those options, a greasy spoon called Bull's. It was a steakhouse that also specialized in ham-based dishes. Mackenzie thought it would be strange to live in a town known primarily for its slaughterhouse and regularly dine at a place like this.

It was one of the main reasons she ordered a Cobb salad for dinner. Ellington had a burger, fries, and a cup of soup. As they dug into their meal, it occurred to her that they had not even really discussed whether or not to go out for dinner. It was an unspoken thing, an assumed decision that took no conversation. She'd heard about this kind of thing between partners before, but they were not partners. This was the first time they had spent any considerable time together, so being able to come to such conclusions in such a way was a little strange.

"I think Bateman is starting to get pissed," Ellington said. "I think he feels like we're showing him up."

"Both of those arrests today were totally haphazard," Mackenzie said. "We weren't actively *seeking* to make those arrests."

"Yeah. But I get where the unrest would come from," Ellington said.

"You know," she said, "I know it might ruffle some feathers in the community, but I think we're getting to the point where we need to just get warrants and search every farm out here. Random unexpected drug busts are fine, but we've still got a man out there that's been kidnapping women."

"It's a thought," he said. "There are eleven farms in a twenty-mile radius."

"Twenty-four if you spread it to fifty miles," she said, one-upping him.

"That's a lot of police work," Ellington said. "Bateman is a pussycat but I don't know how he'd take to that. Especially since we're making him look a little incompetent."

"Well, you and I can narrow it down to four or five," Mackenzie said. "Bring Thorsson and Heideman along. It's a start. Maybe that'll ease Bateman's mind over it."

"Call it in, then," Ellington said. "I think Bateman has a thing for you, anyway."

"No way," she said, between bites of her salad. "I'm pretty sure there's a thing going on between him and Roberts."

"Yeah? How do you know?"

"A woman's intuition, I guess."

"Does that work for nailing ghostlike kidnappers?" he asked. "I guess not, huh?"

"Not so much."

They finished up their dinner and drove back to the Motel 6. On the way, Mackenzie placed the call to Bateman. As Ellington has suggested, Bateman was not an instant fan of the idea.

"Look, Agent White," he said. "I get where you're coming from. I really do. But if you start snooping around people's farms just because we have no other leads, you're going to get some honest and hardworking people riled up. Between you and me…the majority of the farms out here skirt some agricultural laws. Nothing terrible, mind you—just minor infractions. They all know it and probably wouldn't take too kindly to the FBI snooping around."

*Small-town mentality,* she thought. *It might be one of the reasons Bateman and his men were never able to locate the drug sources and make arrests; they were too afraid of stepping on toes and offending locals.*

"Look," he said. "Let me make some calls around and see what I can do. Can we touch base on this in the morning?"

She almost blurted out that waiting for the morning left an entire night for the kidnapper to strike again. Instead, she very calmly asked, "How many cars will be out on patrol tonight?"

"Four at all times. I have some men working sixteen-hour shifts to make it happen."

"Well, give us a call of we can be of service."

Mackenzie ended the call and instantly noticed Ellington's skeptical look. He had pulled into the motel lot, parking the car in front of their rooms. "Um, did you just volunteer me to help with scout duty on the back roads?"

"Maybe." She looked to her watch and added, "That gives us about four and a half hours to sleep."

"Well, before we do I think we should take a look at the topological maps the Bent Creek PD e-mailed me earlier. From what I can see on my phone, they did a great job. They even overlaid the roads onto it from another map. I really want to take a look at those dirt tracks with the chains in front of them."

"Good idea," she said.

They went to Ellington's room, where he synced his phone to the iPad he sometimes carried around for reading and e-mails. As he pulled the maps up on the larger iPad screen, Mackenzie glanced around his room and wondered what it might be like to just stay here when they were done with the maps and coming up with any theories the maps might lead them to.

"Okay," Ellington said, pointing to the screen. "So here are the two little dirt tracks on State Route 14. This one right here dead-ends into what looks like just an empty field. It's pretty damn close to where Mitch Young's trailer is. This other dirt road, though…it looks like it might have branched off into other tracks or dirt roads at some point. See it?"

Mackenzie did see what he was talking about. The dirt track stopped but then, a little bit further up on the map, seemed to pick back up and snake out in three different directions. Eventually, though, they all petered out into nothing.

"No farms back there," she said.

"Well, not currently. But a property owner that may have *once* had a farm back there might be worth looking into."

"So we need to find out who owns the land back there," Mackenzie said. "But if I'm being honest, that feels like a long shot, too."

"Definitely," Ellington said. "But I'm still going to keep kicking every rock I can to see what's underneath."

"Ah, you and your rocks," she said with sigh.

"It's something I've always thought was a good way to look at investigating," Ellington said. "One of the many nuggets of wisdom I took away from my training."

"How long have you been an agent, anyway?" Mackenzie asked.

"This will be my sixth year."

"And have you ever been stumped like this before?"

"A few times," he said. "But in every case but one, we ended up getting our guy."

"What was the one case you didn't?"

Ellington gave her a perplexed look and she nearly recanted the question. But he smiled and sat on the edge of the bed as he started to answer.

"My third year as a field agent, I was tasked with helping track down a guy that was taking pictures of women leaving work, printing them out, and then mailing the pictures to them. Only he had defaced the pictures. Drew pornographic things on them, punched out the eyes in the pictures, that sort of thing. Just as I joined on, he sent a picture to a woman—a mother who had lost her daughter the year before. Her kid went missing and then turned up

78

six weeks later, dead in the Hudson River. The picture the guy sent her was a picture of her daughter. She was wearing the clothes she'd been in on the day she went missing and was bound and gagged in the picture. And that was the last we ever heard from him."

"No more letters after that?" Mackenzie asked.

"Nothing. We looked for that bastard for six months, trying to figure it out, and to this day, we don't have the first clue. I see— shit, never mind."

"No…what? You see what?"

He hesitated for a moment before he continued on. They both sensed that they were breaching some sort of line—going deep in a rather quick fashion.

"I see that picture sometimes," Ellington said. "Of the little girl. She was seven years old. I see the picture he sent the mother sometimes and I want to puke. It makes me sick that we never came close to catching him."

"I guess that case is haunting you right now, isn't it?" she asked.

"Yeah, it is."

She realized that she had subconsciously taken several steps closer to him. She was standing directly in front of him and he looked up at her from his place on the bed. She saw a bit of pain in his eyes as he recounted the story.

Slowly, she reached out to him. She ran her thumb along the side of his face. He took the hand by his face and ran his fingers along the back of it. He then gently pulled her close to him as he stood up.

They were face-to-face now, their noses nearly touching. The pain in his eyes was still there but was fading out. It was replaced by something else, some hopeful energy that made her feel warm.

"Mackenzie," he said. "I don't know if—"

He was interrupted by the ringing of a phone. It was Mackenzie's, still sitting on the table they had viewed the maps on. She let out a shaky breath and chuckled.

"I know, right?" Ellington said, giving her hand a squeeze. "Great timing."

"Probably for the best," she said. She grabbed her phone and suddenly found it very hard to look at him. She made sure she had her senses about her and then answered the phone. "This is Agent White."

"White, it's Bateman. How soon can you and Ellington make it to the hospital?"

"I don't even know where the hospital is," she said. "Why? What's happened?"

"We've found Delores Manning."

# CHAPTER FIFTEEN

Whatever little spark had nearly ignited between Mackenzie and Ellington was instantly put out as she relayed the news of Bateman's call. The news was so monumental that they were able to totally sidestep the awkwardness of the moment as they headed out to the car and then sped to Cedar Rapids, where Delores Manning had been checked in an hour and fifteen minutes ago.

Mackenzie continued to get calls as Ellington drove at speeds near ninety miles an hour toward Cedar Rapids. Some came from Bateman and others came from Agent Thorsson. Thorsson and Heideman had gone back to the Omaha field office earlier in the day and had offered to come back out. Mackenzie had politely declined the assistance, asking only for the details as they came in.

The details were: Two police officers from the Cedar Rapids police department had come to the hospital with Delores Manning. She had been discovered by a switchman at the freight yard on the eastern end of Cedar Rapids. That same switchman had been punched by a vagrant, who was pursued and held by three other switchmen and was then properly arrested once Delores was found in the train car. She'd been badly beaten; the men who found her in the train car assumed she was dead at first.

As Mackenzie and Ellington walked quickly into Mercy Medical Hospital, Ellington stood close to her, whispering softly.

"I've let you lead this thing so far," he said. "Are you okay with this? Questioning a woman who has just come to and is just now realizing what happened to her?"

"Yes, I'll be fine." She knew he was just looking out for her, but she couldn't help but resent the fact that he even had to ask.

After getting Manning's location from the front desk, they took the elevator to the intensive care unit. The moment they stepped out, Mackenzie spotted the two policemen by a door on the far end of the hall. She marched that way, already reaching for her ID. When the policemen saw her and Ellington, she saw the looks of relief on their faces.

"I'm Agent White, and this is Agent Ellington," she said as they all gathered at Delores Manning's door. "How is she?"

"The last report we got from the doctor said that she's come around but is in pain. Her family has been contacted and a grief counselor is due in the next hour or so."

"Do you know if she's in any shape to talk?" Ellington asked.

81

Before either of the cops could answer, a doctor came striding over. He looked tired and a little out of sorts. He also looked a little annoyed that there was such a large group around the doorways of one of his patients.

"I'd rather she not speak right now," the doctor said. "She's out of the woods, yes. But initial CT scans show a mild subarachnoid hemorrhage. If she's too stressed or pushed too hard, there's the risk of a stroke. There's also the very real worry of edema—we'll have to keep an eye on her in the next day or so to stay on top of that. And then there's the minor skull fracture and concussion."

"Does she know what happened to her?" Mackenzie asked.

"Mostly, yes," the doctor said. "She remembers nothing of it, but she knew it as soon as she came to. The vagrant did a number on her. All tests show that the abuse was just the beating. We don't see any signs that she was raped."

*A small relief is still a relief,* Mackenzie thought. "What about where she was before that? Does she remember that?"

"Barely. God, it's terrible. This woman has been through hell," the doctor said. "She's talked about bits and pieces—"

"Doctor, I respect the health and well-being of the patient, as well as your job," Mackenzie said. "But I believe Delores can provide us with information that might possibly lead us to two other women that have been kidnapped in the last few days. I need to speak with her as soon as possible. Of course you can be there. If you feel she's at risk, you can tell me to stop and you'll get no argument from me."

The doctor thought it over for a minute and slumped his shoulders. "At the first sign of distress, you're done. Line your questions up now because I doubt she'll last thirty seconds if she has to recall her trauma. I simply can't risk a stroke."

"Understood," Mackenzie said.

With that, the doctor opened Delores's door and led them inside. The two cops remained at their posts outside the door.

Thankfully, Delores did not look quite as bad as Mackenzie had been expecting. Her head was bandaged heavily on the right side and there was a thin brace around her neck. There was a bruise on the right side of her face and red rings around her eyes that showed she had been crying.

"Delores," the doctor said, "these are agents with the FBI. They want to ask you some questions but I have told them that if you start to react a certain way, I am going to kick them out. Is that okay with you?"

"Yes," Delores said. Her voice was ragged and weak. She looked at Mackenzie and Ellington with hope in her eyes as they came to the left side of the hospital bed.

"Are you up to answering some questions?" Mackenzie asked.

"Yes," she said again. "My head is pounding despite the painkillers, but I'm mostly here."

"I'll be quick," Mackenzie said. "First, you should know that you were one of three women that have been abducted from backwoods roads within the Bent Creek area in the last two weeks. You were the second to be taken from State Route 14. As of right now, we have no idea where the other two women are. Is there *anything* you can tell us about where you were being held before you escaped?"

"Some kind of barn or shed. I heard…grunts, squeals. That kind of thing. Animals maybe. I was being kept in like a box…a container of some kind. Maybe the kind that farmers use to carry animals down highways. Slats in the front."

"Do you remember exactly where you got on the train?"

Delores shook her head. "It all looked the same, from what I can remember. Just trees. I think…yeah, I believe I could actually hear the train horn from time to time when he had me in that box."

"Do you recall how long you ran?" Mackenzie asked.

"No. I mean…it wasn't far. Maybe a mile. Maybe two? I'm just not sure."

"Did you see anything when you escaped?" Mackenzie asked.

"I know I did but I don't really remember. It's all foggy. I remember another barn, I think. And…oh God. I forgot. Until now, I forgot."

"What did you forget?" Ellington asked.

"When I got out of the barn…there was someone else screaming from one of the other barns. A woman. I talked to her briefly…can't remember what I told her. But I didn't have time to save her. I had to get away…"

Delores started weeping and when she did, she grimaced. It seemed to Mackenzie that the act of weeping made her head hurt even worse.

The doctor walked to the door and opened it. "Okay, that's it. She can't—"

"No, it's fine," Delores said. "I don't remember much, anyway."

"We can stop if you need to," Mackenzie said.

Not looking at her, Delores went on. "No, better do it now. Can you believe my damned luck? If I don't spill everything now, who knows what else will happen to me today."

Delores chuckled at her own comment but no one else responded. Delores took a few steadying breaths and went on. "The guy was a big dude. But...I can't remember his face. I'm pretty sure he hit me with a hammer when he took me on the road. Other than that...it's all jumbled and hazy and...shit. I'm so sorry."

"It's okay," Mackenzie said. "By any chance did you get a look at your captor?"

"I think so, but like I said...it's faint. The only face I can clearly recall is the guy on the train..."

Her eyes glazed over here and she looked to the ceiling. Something like shame passed over her face and Mackenzie knew their time with her was over. "I think he tried to rape me but...I don't know. I guess his equipment was malfunctioning." She let out a shrill little laugh at this.

"Delores, thanks for your time," Mackenzie said. "You've given us some great information. Maybe enough to go out and find this guy."

She nodded, the tears still spilling down her cheeks. "If you could throw the asshole from the train in jail, that would be great, too."

"That shouldn't be a problem," Ellington said. "Thanks again."

They both nodded to the doctor and then headed back outside. The cops by the door looked washed out but attentive and doing their best to do their duty.

"The vagrant from the train," Mackenzie said. "Do you guys know where he was taken?"

"Last I heard, he's in a holding cell at headquarters."

"Can you call your supervisor and let him know Agents White and Ellington are headed their way?"

"Yes ma'am," the officer said.

Mackenzie and Ellington walked back toward the elevators. It wasn't until the doors closed in front of them that Ellington spoke up.

"So the police nabbed the vagrant," he said. "Cut and dry. Seems like the Cedar Rapids PD has it wrapped up. Why are we getting involved?"

"Because if we grill him hard enough, he may offer up details he might not find incriminating to himself."

"Such as?"

"Such as where, exactly, he remembers Delores Manning getting on the train. We need to get Bateman on the phone and ask for a detailed map of train routes through Bent Creek, too."

Ellington smiled and gave her a nod. "I'd like to say I thought of that first but...damn, you beat me to it."

# CHAPTER SIXTEEN

Mackenzie stared through the interrogation room glass at the vagrant. So far, he'd told the Cedar Rapids police that his name was Bob Crawford and he was originally from Fort Worth, Texas. But after about an hour of interrogation, that was the only information they were able to get out of him. During the interrogation, they had applied an ice pack to Crawford's hand; he'd apparently busted it up pretty good while beating Delores Manning.

Mackenzie and Ellington were in the observation room with two state cops, both of whom were also looking out at Crawford. One of them looked absolutely furious while the other looked sad and defeated.

"You mind if I take a crack at him?" Mackenzie asked.

"Be my guest," said the angry-looking state cop. "But I'm telling you right now, the guy is worthless. He's got the shakes and he smells like a mixture between a locker room and the floor of a bar. He's jonesing for a drink and can't even think straight. If you can't get anything out of him, we'll probably just toss him in the drunk tank until the morning."

"Thanks," Mackenzie said. She left the observation room and walked out into the hallway. Just as she was reaching for the door that led to the interrogation room, she heard Ellington falling in behind her.

"You got this?" he asked.

"Yes, I'll be fine."

They shared a stare for a moment and in it, she understood what he meant. This vagrant, supposedly named Bob Crawford, had beaten the hell out of Delores Manning. While he had not raped her, the evidence indicated that he had tried but ultimately failed. Ellington was simply making sure Mackenzie wasn't so repulsed by the creep that it would affect her judgment and skills.

"You mind if I sit in?" he asked.

"If you want," she said.

Without waiting for his response, she opened the door and walked inside. Bob Crawford was facing the door and when she entered the room, he made no attempt to hide his shock. A lazy grin crossed his face—a grin which dropped completely when Ellington joined her.

Ellington stood by the door as Mackenzie took the single seat on the other side of the table. "Mr. Crawford," she said, "I'm Agent

White with the FBI. I'm really hoping you're going to be more cooperative with me than you were with the police."

He looked down at the table and Mackenzie saw that he was indeed trembling as the state cop had said.

"You're shaking," she pointed out. "You okay?"

"I need a drink," Crawford said. "Any chance you can help me out with that?"

"What you need is some hard time in prison," she said. "You messed that woman up quite badly. Can I ask why?"

He shrugged. "I was weak."

"Weak?"

"It's been forever since I've been with a woman."

Anger flared up in Mackenzie but she kept it down. "Well, it seems like your plans didn't really pan out well, huh? Couldn't concentrate? Was the train making too much noise? Did you fuck your hand up too bad to get a hard-on?"

Crawford's face flushed with anger and shame. He stopped trembling for just a moment and was now looking directly at her.

"Mr. Crawford, did the police tell you who this woman was or what she had been through in the last few days?"

"No."

"She escaped from a man that we believe held her captive for at least two days. And then once she does something heroic and manages to escape, you come along and make it even worse for her. What the hell were you doing in that train anyway?"

"Traveling," he said. "I don't exactly have a car. I haven't had a job in almost six years...just shit work on farms that last about a day. I haven't had any real employment or friends or family in—"

"You can spare me the wandering vagrant sob story," Mackenzie said. "There are tons of people down on their luck that don't beat and attempt to rape women."

Crawford had no response to that. He focused on the table once again, cutting his eyes toward Ellington as if looking for backup.

"Mr. Crawford," Mackenzie said, "do you happen to know where the train was when this woman got on?"

It was clear that he did not intend to speak. He slouched his shoulders and sank down in the chair a bit. The moment he did this, Mackenzie got to her feet and shrugged.

"Have it your way. Remember me when you're in a holding cell, though. You'll be there for at least three days while paperwork is shuffled around. No one is going to rush to process a vagrant. And I can tell you right now without a doubt that you're looking at two years minimum. And if you think getting a drink is hard *now*, wait until you're in prison. I hear the toilet bowl wine tastes like piss and gasoline."

She headed for the door, catching the bewildered look on Ellington's face. She then heard Crawford moving in the chair behind her.

"Wait," he said. "Look…I just hopped on the train and went. I've done it five times in all. I don't know where the hell I am half of the time."

Mackenzie turned around to face him again. "Fair enough," she said. "But what can you remember seeing when she jumped onto the train car?"

"Not much, really. Just trees. Some pines for sure, but I don't know much of anything else."

"Pines along the edge of the tracks?" she asked.

"Yeah, I think so. Pretty sure there was a grove of pines."

"And that's it?" Mackenzie asked. "You're certain?"

"Pretty sure, yeah."

"Thank you," Mackenzie said and exited the room.

She and Ellington huddled together outside of the room, standing between the doors to the interrogation room and the observation room.

"I won't lie," Ellington said. "I sort of like that side of you."

"I don't," she said. "It makes me feel a little too out of control."

"Pines," Ellington said. "That could be a huge break."

"It could. That clue along with a working map of today's train routes within the area could pay off huge. Can you make the call to Bateman while I wrap things up in here?"

"Sure," he said. "And Mackenzie…I mean *White*. That really was impressive. How the hell did you get him to open up like that?"

"He beat the hell out of a woman today…which makes me think he's bullied and devalued women all of his life. When one gets into his face in an unabashed way, his habits and formerly held beliefs shut down and he's left with nothing more than basic panic to work with."

Ellington smiled and nodded as he pulled out his cell phone.

"Oh, and Ellington…ask Bateman if there's anyone new in town. This whole drifter and vagabond thing has me thinking that there's a chance this guy might not be a local. If he's drifting through town under everyone's radar, he'd have hiding spots no one would ever think of. It's a slim chance but worth a try."

"Can do," Ellington said, pulling up Bateman's number.

Mackenzie wasted no time soaking in his appreciation. She entered the observation room with all cylinders clicking, already formulating a plan for when they returned to Bent Creek.

## CHAPTER SEVENTEEN

They were on the road back to Bent Creek for less than ten minutes when Mackenzie received a call from Sheriff Bateman. It was nearing eight o'clock and Mackenzie felt like the entire day had slipped through her fingers. It was an exhausting feeling but it also served to offer a bit of motivation, too.

"So," Bateman said. "Ellington asked if we had any new guys in town. My first reaction was *no*, but the more I thought about it, this one guy did come to mind. I wouldn't go so far as to call him a drifter by any means, but we ran his record and saw that he's lived in six different towns over the last two years. He's got a bit of a record, too: possession of marijuana with intent to sell, petty theft, and several traffic violations."

"Got a name and address?" Mackenzie asked.

"The name is Miller Rooney. I'll text the address over to you. I can have a few guys meet you over there if you want."

"I don't think that'll be necessary," Mackenzie said. "But thanks as always for the help."

Bateman gave a little noise of acknowledgment and then hung up the phone. Mackenzie set her own phone down on the car console and frowned.

"I think we're starting to get on Bateman's nerves," she said.

"How's that?" Ellington asked from behind the wheel.

"I'm not sure. I think he feels like he's not being very much help. Maybe we're starting to step on his toes…making his force look bad."

Ellington only shrugged in response. Meanwhile, Mackenzie's phone dinged as she received the text from Bateman with the address to one Miller Rooney.

"Feel like making one more stop tonight?" she asked.

"Do I have a choice?" he asked.

"No."

She plugged the address into the GPS and they headed to yet another lead, this one feeling just as flimsy as the others. *Maybe it won't all be for nothing,* Mackenzie thought with a sense of dry humor. *Maybe we'll end up with another unintentional drug bust that will piss Bateman off even more.*

\*\*\*

It was 8:55 by the time they reached the address Bateman had given them. It was a basic one-story house, tucked in along the woods with other houses. If this guy was indeed just drifting through, Mackenzie assumed he was renting the place. Being so late, she nearly suggested that they wait to pay the guy a visit tomorrow. But they were already here and the day had already taken its toll—so what was one more stop?

Ellington pulled the car into the small unkempt driveway and killed the lights. When Mackenzie stepped out into the night and faced the house, she was reminded of approaching Mitch Young's trailer. She wasn't getting the same foreboding feeling as she had then but the atmosphere of small-town life, surrounded by trees at night, was unsettling nonetheless.

Ellington knocked on the door. When it was answered, it took both Mackenzie and Ellington a moment to speak up. They weren't exactly expecting such a scene when the door opened.

A young woman answered the door. She looked to be in her early to mid-twenties. She was wearing a T-shirt that had been modified into a tank top, the sleeves having been cut off. The makeshift tank top clung tightly to her, pressing the Rolling Stones logo tightly across her small but prominent breasts, the sides of which spilled generously out of the sides. Other than the shirt, she wore nothing but a pair of black panties. Her blonde hair spilled over her shoulders in a mess that somehow looked great on her.

"Yeah?" she asked, apparently unashamed of her appearance.

"We're looking for Miller Rooney," Mackenzie said, still taken aback by the girl's state of dress.

"Yeah," the girl said again, turning slowly. "Hold up. I'll get him."

Two things occurred to Mackenzie as the girl turned away. First, she was stoned out of her mind. Second, the black panties clung to the girl's rear as if they had been spray painted on. She looked over at Ellington and was impressed that he was not taking the moment to appreciate the view.

"Thoughts?" Mackenzie whispered as the girl went further back into the small house.

"It's blasphemy to ruin a Rolling Stones shirt like that," Ellington said. "Also…I think she's pretty baked."

Seconds later, a young man came to the door. He was shirtless and wore only a pair of jeans that were torn at the knees. His long hair was parted down the middle and tucked behind his ears. Mackenzie thought he looked a bit like a dark-haired version of Kurt Cobain.

"You're looking for me?" he asked.

"Yes, we are," Mackenzie said. "We're agents White and Ellington with the FBI. We were hoping to have a word with you."

Miller gave a quick glance over his shoulder, probably nervous about having whatever drugs his girlfriend was high on. Without inviting them in, Miller turned on his porch light and stepped outside, closing the door behind him.

"Sure, what's up?" he asked. "FBI…really?"

"Yes," Mackenzie said. "And I assure you that we aren't here to snoop around in whatever kind of chemical-induced party you and your lady friend are involved in. I'd actually like to ask you about why you've come to Bent Creek."

"Oh, sure, sure," Miller said. Mackenzie thought Miller might also be a little stoned, though not as much as the girl who had answered the door. "Well, Kelly's parents live here. Her dad was thinking he could get me a job at the slaughterhouse, but that didn't really work out."

"Kelly…is that the girl that answered the door?" Mackenzie asked.

"Yeah, that's her."

"Why did things not work out with the job?" Ellington asked.

"Hey, man…wait, why are you guys even here?"

*Yeah, stoned off his ass,* Mackenzie thought. *He can't even put his own thoughts together coherently.*

"We're here because there are a few people that have gone missing over the last few days," Mackenzie said. "Please don't take offense to this, but in cases like this it is usually a good idea to speak to someone who just showed up in town."

"Oh, no doubt," Miller said, nodding as if he had just been told some huge truth. "Well, the job didn't work out because of my background check. I got a record. Nothing bad, you know? But people are so fucking choosy. Like I'm not good enough to work in a slaughterhouse."

"How much longer will you stay here in Bent Creek?" Mackenzie asked.

"Who knows? I've been helping out on one of the pig farms for a bit. It sucks, but it's money. Kelly is pissed at her folks. We might head back out to Seattle in a few weeks."

Mackenzie felt confident that Miller Rooney was not the man they were looking for. Not only was he not smart enough, but someone with such a reckless and carefree attitude would not have the patience or durability to kidnap someone…much less three people.

"Well, that'll be all," Mackenzie said. "Thanks for your time. And Mr. Rooney…be a little more discreet about the drug use, okay? If I wanted to be a bitch, I could send the cops over right now and bust you. Got it?"

Alarm lit up Miller's eyes for a moment. "Yeah, damn. Sorry. Yeah, I'll do that."

Mackenzie and Ellington stepped down off of the small porch and headed back to the car. As Ellington backed out of the driveway, Mackenzie watched Miller Rooney slip back into his house.

"Well, that was a monumental waste of time," Ellington said.

"Not a total waste of time," Mackenzie said. "It gave me some great ideas of how to repurpose the few band T-shirts I held on to from my teenage years."

"Oh, don't *even* tease me like that," Ellington said with a laugh that was a little too forced to be real.

"I think I need a drink," she said.

"Yeah, I could do a drink. You're buying this time, right?"

"Sure," she said. "Before we make any plans, though, I should check in with Bateman. He's been bending over backwards for us. The least I can do is keep him in the loop and see if there's anything else we can do for him."

"With all these drug busts, I'd say we're doing enough," Ellington said.

Mackenzie felt the same way but didn't want to seem quite as indignant. She placed the call to Bateman and noticed that he sounded a little frustrated when he answered.

"This is Bateman," he answered.

"We just spoke with Miller Rooney and it's pretty clear he's not involved in this. How are things there? Any luck on those train maps and schedules?"

"Some," he said. "Right now we're working on trying to determine where a row of pines might be that close to the tracks. I've placed a call to the Forestry Department, but we won't hear from them until tomorrow morning."

"Don't hesitate if you need anything."

"Same to you," he said, but it was clear that he didn't really mean it.

Over the course of the last two days, something had happened that had shifted his attitude. Mackenzie wondered if it was the mere fact that she and Ellington were showing him up and running things here. Or maybe he was feeling just as lost and defeated as she was.

She hated to feel so passive about making very little progress on the case—especially after Delores Manning had managed to escape—but she also knew that there was nothing she could do. The idea of returning to the files on her father's case popped up in her head but that was somehow even more depressing. So for now, she was fine with wasting an hour or two at the bar with Ellington.

She supposed there were worse ways to spend downtime on a case that seemed to have no leads, clues, or end in sight.

# CHAPTER EIGHTEEN

They returned to the Bent Creek Bar, receiving their first drinks at 9:30. Mackenzie was tired and hoped a few drinks would ensure that she'd sleep well tonight. She knew that if she returned to her room with the least bit of energy, she'd end up with her nose buried in her father's files. And that would mean a restless night's sleep that would be plagued with nightmares.

There was surprisingly little conversation between them. What *was* discussed was not nearly as serious and businesslike as Mackenzie had pictured Ellington to be. It made her feel irresponsible, but she also needed it. The last true friend she'd had was no longer in the bureau—she had, in fact, left the academy just after graduation. It had been a very long time since Mackenzie had just been able to speak to someone about nonsense.

"So," Ellington said. "These band T-shirts that you are going to make a lot sexier…what bands are we talking about?"

"Oh, we don't need to go there."

"But we do. What have you learned about me this week? For starters, I like the Stones and I hate Skynyrd. That's all you need to know about a man right there. So now it's your turn."

"I may or may not still own a Nine Inch Nails shirt."

"Really? I did *not* peg you as a former goth."

"I wasn't. I just liked that kind of music. "

"That's a relief," Ellington said. "I had you pegged as one of those boy bands freaks."

"In other words, you think very little of me."

"That's so far from the truth you can't even see it," he said. "What I've seen out of you these last few days has been remarkable. I knew you were good—I knew it from the first time I saw you in Nebraska—but you're an exceptional agent. McGrath thinks so, too."

"Well, I'm not feeling like it right now," she said.

"I think the maps and train info we get will help," he said.

Mackenzie noticed that her beer was empty but rather than ordering another, she stood up. She dropped a ten on the bar to pay for their drinks. "I'm going to call it a night," she said. "I'm incredibly tired and I can't remember the last time I got more than six hours of sleep."

"More than six hours?" Ellington said. "You're telling me it can be done?"

He finished off his own beer and got up with her. "Well, I'm not drinking alone. And there's worse ways to punch a clock."

They left the Bent Creek Bar together, heading back across the parking lot to the Motel 6. Ellington remained with her as she walked to her room. She pulled the room key out of her pocket and put it into the lock, wondering if he was waiting for an invitation to come inside.

"You did great today, White. If I may be so bold, I'd like to make a prediction. We will catch this guy within the next forty-eight hours."

"That *is* pretty bold," she said.

"Optimistic," he said. With that, he smiled and said, "Goodnight, Mackenzie."

He walked to his door the next room over and gave her a little wave. Mackenzie unlocked her own door and stepped into her room. She held the key in her hands for a moment as a thought came to her mind. Actually, it wasn't so much a thought as it was an *urge.*

*A bold statement,* she thought.

Pocketing her key, she walked back out into the night and approached Ellington's door. She knocked twice and waited. She heard him moving around inside, coming for the door. When he opened it, he looked a little confused.

"Everything okay?" he asked.

"Yeah," she said. "I was just thinking about another bold statement."

Before he could ask her what she meant, she stepped into his room and kissed him.

It took him a moment to understand what was happening but when he did, he returned it. The kiss was quick and urgent, a five-second connection that they both broke at the same time. They stood there, about a foot away from one another, sizing each other up.

*He's going to give me the "I'm not into you like that" speech now,* Mackenzie thought. *Oh my God, how did I read this so wrong?*

But then he was stepping toward her. He placed one hand on her hip and the other along the side of her neck. There was the slightest hesitation between them before they were kissing again. This one was a bit slower but no less urgent. What she had *not* expected was how quickly they both sank into it. This second kiss was not awkward at all. It was fluid, there was an undeniable heat in it, and, if she was being honest with herself, it was sexy as hell.

From the expert way he kissed her, their tongues meeting and their lips never breaking from one another, to the way his hand gripped her hip, it was nearly perfect. It was so perfect that she wasn't aware that he had gently pressed her against the wall until she felt it pressing lightly against her shoulders.

She let her lips and her hands control her in that moment. She finally broke the kiss, but only to place her mouth on his jaw, and then his neck. Her hands, meanwhile, found the buttons on his shirt and started to undo them. In response, he started to do the same. As he worked at her buttons, his hands slipped beneath her shirt and she felt like some anxious little school girl as a shudder passed through her.

With both of their shirts open, she felt flesh on flesh. She drew him closer to her, pressing him against her. There was now more than heat to their kiss, but some sort of spark that she had not expected, some building tension that had been slowly forming between them since she had first seen him in Nebraska almost a year ago.

She trailed her hand down his sides, then she was grazing his chest and going for the button of his pants.

He stepped back, pulling away. The kiss had been so intense that he was out of breath. He was looking at her with a conflicted expression. She saw want and raw lust in his eyes, but there was something else, too.

"Mackenzie," he said. "I can't even believe I'm about to say this, but…I can't."

"What is it?" she asked. She had no intentions whatsoever of pleading with him but she could not remember being so physically drawn to anyone before. She was still reeling from the kiss; she felt like there was a slight tilt to the floor.

"Trust me," he said, "I want to. I've wanted to for quite some time. But…I can't be that guy. My divorce was just finalized a few weeks ago. If we go through with this right now—"

"Oh, I see," she said. And she *did* see. But it did nothing to subdue the frustration it made her feel. She started to slowly button her shirt back up, doing her best not to seem like she was pouting.

"I should have stopped it sooner," he said, starting to button his own shirt. "But my God, Mackenzie…I've been wanting to kiss you for longer than I care to admit."

"I know the feeling," she said. And she decided that would be the end of it. She was not going to say anything else about it. As far as she was concerned, she could wake up tomorrow and go on living as if the last minute or so of her life had never happened.

"I'm sorry," he said.

"Don't be. I started it. It's okay, Ellington," she said, making sure to use his last name as a way to show him that she was going to be all business from here on out. "I'm just going to head back to my room and go to sleep. More than six hours, remember?"

He nodded. She looked directly at him for the first time since he had pushed away from her. The fact that he looked at odds with himself made her feel a little better. At least it wasn't just her that was torn over what had just happened.

"Goodnight," she said, opening his door and making her exit.

Ellington returned her *good night* but the door closed between them before he could get it all out.

***

She again felt massively immature as she tried going to bed. She was sexually frustrated and visions of Ellington with his shirt unbuttoned would not leave her mind. She nearly got out of bed to return to the few files she had regarding her father but fought the urge. She managed to fall asleep shortly before midnight, the toll of the day finally catching up to her.

In her sleep, she recognized the edges of a nightmare creeping in. She'd had so many of them over the last eighteen years or so that her sleeping mind was aware of them before they got started. In the quiet of her motel room, she let out a little moan of fear in her sleep.

In this nightmare, she was standing in the middle of a large field. The house she had grown up in for most of her childhood stood in front of her but behind that, there were the thick woods of Iowa, the forests that surrounded State Route 14. As she stared at the house, she heard someone approaching from behind her.

She turned and saw her father standing there—alive and unharmed. He smiled at her and placed an arm around her.

"You look like you're lost," he said.

"I feel lost," she admitted.

"This place," he said, gesturing toward the house, "will always be your home. You've gone here and there since I've been gone, but you always come back here, don't you?"

She looked to the house and realized that she hated it with the same ferocity one might hate another human being.

"I come back for you," she said.

"I know," Benjamin White said. He then reached into the pocket of his pants and pulled out a business card. When he handed

98

it to her, Mackenzie was not at all surprised to see that it was the business card for Barker Antiques.

"I don't know what this means," she said.

"You will. Just don't give up on me, kid."

He then reached behind him and pulled something out of the waistband of his pants. He showed it to her and she jumped back. He held a Colt .44 revolver in his hand—the exact type of revolver that was believed to have killed him. Slowly, he brought the gun to his head.

"I'll be here until you figure it all out," he said, grazing the barrel of the Colt against his head. "But I also feel like I'm the reason you keep coming back here...coming back here and forgetting about people like her."

When he said *her,* he nodded to the front porch of the house. There, she saw Delores Manning, splayed out on the steps. She was clearly dead, covered in an excessive amount of blood.

"Daddy, I'm so lost."

"Then find yourself," he said.

She opened her mouth to argue but the thunderous report from the Colt seemed to shake the day. In a spray of red, her father crumpled to his knees and fell face down on the grass.

Mackenzie screamed and went to her knees. Her scream tore through the nightmare like a screeching wind, but was not quite as loud as the thunderous echo of the gunshot that had claimed her father.

# CHAPTER NINETEEN

Missy Hale watched the first snowflake plop against the windshield and said, "Shit."

It was bad enough that she was starting her day out incredibly early, but the snow in the forecast was just the icing on the cake. There had been enough snow in the last few days of her travels and as far as she was concerned, spring could not get here fast enough.

Maybe if she could get through her next stop quick enough, she could be back in Des Moines by eleven o'clock. She'd made the day's big stop, at the Bent Creek Slaughterhouse, at 7:45. Now as the morning crept toward 9:00, she had one stop left to make—some small-time farmer who had been dodging the government on waste regulations for months now. As a researcher and liaison for the Department of Agriculture, dealing with waste was definitely one of the more humbling parts of Missy's job. There were some days when she needed to take two showers just to make sure she got the stench of pig and cow manure out of her hair.

Another snowflake hit her windshield, then another. She came to the end of the long access road that led to the slaughterhouse and put on her right turn signal. She started down the road, glancing over to the street address of the next farm. It was on the other side of Bent Creek but she knew the area well enough to know that she could take a quick detour off of the main highway, taking State Route 14 out to the opposite side of town.

Missy drove for another five miles, getting closer to the actual signs of life within the little town of Bent Creek. The snow was still whispering down and the skies overhead showed signs of something much more significant in the next few hours.

When she was less than half a mile away from her turn-off onto State Route 14, she caught a glimpse of a flashing red light on the side of the road just ahead. She slowed down and looked in that direction as she approached the light. She came to what looked like the entrance to what had once been a service road or basic rural dirt road. There was a truck pulled into it, about ten feet off of the road. The driver's side door was open and a man was bent over inside, his legs out on the ground but the rest of him hidden. From what she could tell, he looked very still. That, plus the flashing of the hazard lights, raised an alarm.

Slowly, she pulled over to the side of the road, coming in behind the truck. Closer to the truck, Missy could now see that the man's legs were limp. She had no idea what had happened here, but the man was hurt. Maybe he'd been out driving, had some kind of heart episode or massive headache, and pulled over to the side of the road, hoping his hazards would attract someone.

She got out of her service truck—a standard model for the Iowa Department of Agriculture—and pulled her coat's hood up. She hated even the feel of the damned snowflakes falling on her cheeks and nose.

"Hello?" she said. "Can you hear me? Are you okay?"

She took another step forward and started to feel uneasy.

*If you think he's hurt and want to help, call 911 from your cell phone. Just...get back into your truck.*

But the limp stature of those legs told her that this man was seriously hurt. She should at least check his condition before calling. The person on the other end at 911 would ask for details anyway.

"Sir?" she said, stepping forward. She could now see into the truck. The man had a hood pulled over his head, joined to a thick coat. "Are you okay?"

And then, in a flash, the man moved.

She screamed but only for a moment. Something hard hit her in the center of the forehead and everything in her body shut down temporarily. She got a look at the man for just a second before she went to the ground in a whirl of blackness.

\*\*\*

He'd been careful this time. He'd checked the schedule and had a pretty good idea of when the woman would come out of the slaughterhouse. He'd worked there before—he had even seen Missy Hale a few times while on staff. So he knew she'd be done by 8:45 or 9:00. He'd parked here, knowing that no one would recognize the old pickup truck. It had been sitting on his property for two years, under a tarp. The farm-use tags on it were fakes and while they could be traced, they'd be traced to some poor sap in North Carolina.

He'd seen her truck coming down the road and played dead, making sure to put the hazards on. He knew she'd pull in behind him, which would make getting out of here a little difficult.

And then, of course, he thought he might have hit her far too hard. He'd used a simple hammer, striking her with the edge of the head. He'd expected her to get woozy, not to black out completely.

But it was done now and he couldn't change it. So he had to work with what he had.

He also knew that while traffic on this road was practically non-existent after 8:00, he had to anticipate the occasional stray or wandering car. So he had to move his ass.

He looked at his watch as he started for State Route 14. From the moment Missy had pulled in behind him to his return to the main road, less than ninety seconds had passed. Ahead and behind, there was no traffic on the road.

The snow was coming down faster now. While others would bemoan the snow, he was happy to have it. It covered everything, washed everything away.

Hopefully, it had covered up any evidence Delores Manning had left behind during her run through the forests yesterday. He supposed there was a chance that she had told the authorities everything she could. He fully expected the police to show up at any moment. And if they did, that was fine. He was ready for them. Hell…maybe they'd even understand why he was doing it.

If not, though, he had plenty of ammunition.

Besides, as beautiful as the snow was and as excited as he got about a confrontation with the police, he had more pressing things to worry about for the moment.

For instance, he could not wait to shove Missy Hale into the very same container that had held Delores Manning until yesterday morning.

He had a ton of work to do first, though. With a confident grin spread across his face, he went to work as the pelting snow thickened around him.

# CHAPTER TWENTY

With no alarm set, Mackenzie slept in until 7:20. While it was still relatively early, she certainly considered it sleeping in. More than that, it was more than six hours, as she and Ellington had joked about last night.

*Ah hell...Ellington,* she thought. *I guess I need to face him at some point this morning.*

She sat up in bed and grabbed her phone. She had no missed texts, no calls, no e-mails. She realized that if no new leads turned up today, she and Ellington could very well be headed back to DC by the end of the day. She got out of bed and prepared herself for the day, working on an automated schedule: shower, teeth, hair, get dressed. She had it down to a science, able to get it all done in right at twenty minutes.

When she was done, she figured she'd sidestep the awkwardness with Ellington altogether. She'd knock on his door and they'd head out to face the day together. With no new leads, she figured they'd get started at the Bent Creek PD. She wondered if Thorsson and Heideman would be there or if they were still back at the field office due to a lack of results.

She stepped outside and as she closed the door behind her she saw Ellington coming out of the motel office. He gave her a wave and came over to her, pulling the car keys out of his pocket.

"What were you doing in there?" she asked.

"I got the call from McGrath this morning. He asked for an update and I gave it to him. He's asked that we report back to DC no later than tonight if we can't turn anything up today. He'll keep us on the case but he doesn't want to keep us out here on a case that's showing no progress."

Mackenzie had assumed this would happen, so it came as no real surprise. "Want to head down to see Bateman?" she asked. "Maybe we'll be able to pull something from the maps and the train routes."

"Sounds good," he said. "Listen...about last night—"

She shook her head. "Nope. No need to go there. Let's see if we can make today productive and wrap this case up. I won't be able to do that if I keep thinking about last night."

"Fair enough," he said.

She hadn't meant to sound like a bitch but she knew it had come off that way. Hopefully, Ellington knew her well enough to know that was not her intent. It was hard to tell because neither of them said a single word in the two minutes it took—even in the new snow—to get from the Motel 6 to the Bent Creek police department.

When they arrived at the station, they made their way to the back after being directed there by the receptionist. Mackenzie smelled coffee and donuts—scents that perked her up despite the tension between her and Ellington and McGrath requesting them back in DC. She knocked on the conference room door, which was partially open, and got a rushed "Come on in."

When she entered, Bateman gave her half a wave and a thin smile. He looked tired and, quite honestly, not too happy to see her.

"Agents White and Ellington," Bateman said. He pointed to an older man, around sixty or so, and said, "This is Earl Temper from the Forestry Department. He's working to narrow down the locations we believe Delores Manning could have gotten on that train."

"Any luck so far?" Mackenzie asked.

"A bit," Earl said. "Fortunately, there aren't a whole lot of pines in the woods around here, so it makes my job a bit easier. He slid a forestry map over to her and pointed a finger at a U-shaped mark he had placed on the map with a marker.

"That right there is an area of about twenty miles, all running right alongside the tracks. As far as I know, it's the only area there'd be pines that close to the tracks, but I'm making some calls and requesting some data to make sure I'm right. If you give me an hour or so, I can probably knock that twenty-mile radius down to about five or ten."

"That would be great," Mackenzie said.

Meanwhile, Officer Roberts slid one of three boxes of donuts toward Mackenzie and Ellington. "Help yourself," she said.

Mackenzie did, giving her thanks, but she was a little weirded out. Something had changed in this place since yesterday. Something about it all seemed very *Twin Peaks* now and she wasn't quite sure why. Maybe it was just Bateman's mood or the tension between her and Ellington, but something was definitely off.

"Is there a history of any other types of crimes out in that area?" Mackenzie asked, looking down at Earl's map.

"Nope," Bateman said. "I had someone check that out about twenty minutes before you guys showed up."

She wasn't sure if this was a deliberate jab or not. As it turned out, she didn't have a lot of time to dwell on it. Directly after Bateman said this, his cell phone rang. He took it off of the clip on his belt and answered it through a mouthful of donut.

"This is Bateman."

He listened to the call for a moment and then sat straight up in his chair. Mackenzie tried to read his expression but wasn't sure if he was receiving good news or bad news.

"One second," Bateman said. "I'm going to put you on speaker." Before he did, he addressed everyone in the conference room—Mackenzie, Ellington, Roberts, and Earl Temper—and said: "This is Janice Smith from the Department of Agriculture."

He then placed the phone on speaker mode and set it in the middle of the table. "Okay, Janice…you've got me, Earl Temper from the Forestry Department, Officer Roberts, and Agents White and Ellington from the FBI. Tell them what you just told me and then finish the details."

"Sure," said Smith. "I got a call from one of your local famers down there…a gentleman named David Ayers. He had a meeting with a rep from the Department of Agriculture this morning. He's met with her several times and she's always prompt and on time. He called us about ten minutes ago to say that the rep—Missy Hale—had not yet shown up. We've tried calling her cell phone and there is no answer. Now, I know it might be a stretch, but I know about the trouble you've been having down there with the disappearances. I thought it might be something worth looking into. I've already mailed over all of Missy's info as well as the license and registration information on the truck she's driving."

"We'll certainly look into it," Bateman said, giving Mackenzie a look as if to say *I hope that's okay with you.* She gave him a nod to indicate that it was.

"Thanks," Smith said. "Honestly, it's just not like Missy to be late or, at the very least, to not make a call saying she's running behind. Otherwise, I wouldn't have bothered calling."

"That's fine," Bateman said. "We'll be sure to keep you posted."

With that, he ended the call and looked around the conference room. "I think she's right," he said. "It might seem like a stretch, but what other leads do we have at this point?"

"I don't think it's too much of a stretch," Mackenzie said. "Without any reports of car accidents that would delay her, any missing person case in an area where there have been multiple similar cases is worth looking into."

She started for the door without another word. As she did, Bateman also stood up. "At the risk of crowding the scene, I think I'd like to join you on this one."

"Of course," Mackenzie said. She didn't want to waste any more of her time or attention trying to figure out why things seemed to be tense with Bateman. Besides, if he wanted to come along, he had every right to do so.

She even let him lead the way, pausing as he stopped to grab another donut before he left the conference room. As Mackenzie left the room, she was overcome with a strange feeling; while she certainly hoped Missy Hale was alive and well and this was all an overreaching mix-up, she also knew that if she *was* in danger, this could be the last lead to pursue before she and Ellington had to call it quits and head back home.

## CHAPTER TWENTY ONE

When they arrived at David Ayers's farm, Mackenzie saw that he was placing a tarp over a stack of firewood along the left side of his nice two-story farmhouse. The snow was really coming down, making Mackenzie wonder just how deep it would need to get before Bateman had someone put chains on the tires of his patrol car. Mackenzie noticed the tail end of the cop car in front of her and Ellington slipping slightly to the left as it came to a stop in Ayers's driveway.

Ayers looked out at them and gave a wave as he tightened his hood up over his head. He walked slowly to the porch, waiting for everyone to join him. Roberts had come along with Bateman, leading a few steps ahead of Mackenzie and Bateman. When introductions were made all around, Ayers welcomed them into his house.

It was a gorgeous farmhouse, rustic to the point of being classy. A wood-burning fireplace roared below the mantel in the spacious living room.

"I have to say," Ayers said, "I didn't think my call would cause such a fuss. I certainly wasn't expecting the FBI."

"Well, the Department of Agriculture called me soon after you called to ask about Missy Hale," Bateman said. "As you probably know, we've had a string of disappearances in the area. The people at the Department of Agriculture don't want to take any chances. No one can get Missy on her phone, e-mail, nothing."

"Oh my God," Ayers said.

"So...I know it's a long shot," Bateman said, "but can you think of anything that might have been said between the two of you that we'd need to know?"

"Missy and I?" Ayers asked. "No. She comes by every quarter to do a check on how I'm handling the waste procedures...making sure it's not threatening local water supplies and things like that. We have a friendly chat when she comes over but that's about it."

"You didn't speak to her about this visit?" Mackenzie asked. "No conversations about setting up the appointment?"

"No, none at all. It's all done online. I knew it was Missy that would be coming again because it was her name on my invoice."

"Could we see that invoice, please?" Mackenzie asked.

"Sure," he said. "It's in my office. Give me one second."

The four authorities sat by quietly as Ayers stepped away to his office. When he was out of earshot, Mackenzie stepped closer to Bateman so that she could speak quietly.

"How well do you know David Ayers?"

"Pretty good. If you're wanting to know if I think he's capable of kidnapping women, the answer is absolutely not. The guy doesn't have any sort of record. His wife passed five or six years ago and although he's wealthy enough to retire, he keeps working. He's one of the nicest folks in town if you ask me."

"Has his farm been around for a while?" she asked.

"Yeah. One of the first in town, I think. I don't know the family history or anything, but I think it's been here since the 1920s or so."

She had no more questions, which was just as well, since Ayers came walking back in. He handed Mackenzie a sheet of paper with a basic form on it. It gave the date and time of today's visit. A small note near the bottom said *Your meeting is with representative Missy Hale. Contact this office with any questions.*

"Mr. Ayers," Mackenzie said, "given her job, I wonder if there were any other farms in town that might have had issues with her? Maybe she gave someone a bad review or slapped a fine on someone? Can you think of anyone that resented her?"

"No, but I guess it's a possibility."

"Hey, David," Bateman said. "Do you know if the state still sends them out in those God-awful trucks?"

"The beige-colored short-bodies?" Ayers asked.

"Those are the ones."

"The last time she came out, yeah."

Mackenzie made a note of this. They had the license plate number, the registration number, and now, potentially, the color of the truck. It was quite possibly the strongest lead they had. From the information Bateman had, they also knew that Missy had made the early-morning appointment she'd had with the slaughterhouse. So that meant somewhere between the slaughterhouse and the Ayers farm, a very distinct truck had somehow gone missing.

*Now we're getting somewhere,* she thought.

But the snow was still falling outside and would almost certainly hinder any sort of search.

"Thank you for your time, Mr. Ayers," she said. "I'll leave you in the highly capable hands of Sheriff Bateman and Officer Roberts. Agent Ellington and I need to get going."

Bateman looked at her with a confused expression—one that nearly mirrored the one on Ellington's face. Always on top of things, though, Ellington nodded and followed her to the door. He said nothing to her until they were down the porch stairs and headed for their rental car.

"You worried about the snow, too?" he asked.

"Yes. If we want to find that truck, we need to do it before the snow makes it impossible. You have any idea what the forecast is?"

He pulled out his cell phone and opened his weather app as they got into the car. "Flurries for another hour or so and then it's going to be picking up."

"So we *really* have to do this quickly," she said. "We know that Missy Hale was at the slaughterhouse this morning. So let's start there and trace every route there is between there and here. That truck has to be somewhere."

"Does it?" Ellington asked as he backed out of the driveway. "Let's say our guy did take Missy Hale. Why would he take her vehicle when he left the others on the side of the road?"

"Because if he *did* take her, this was in the morning. Daytime. His other scenes have all occurred at night."

"And honestly," he argued, "that's why I don't think Missy is one of his victims. Why would he stray from his norm? Why take the risk?"

"Because Delores Manning escaped. He was hurt. Hs pride, his ego, whatever. Not only did he need to replace her, but he needs to do something more daring to prove something to himself."

"Shit," Ellington said. "You're right. That's a good point."

"I'm thinking he either has her truck or he left it on the side of the road like the others. I think we should maybe request a few of Bateman's guys to run down State Route 14 since that seems to be the suspect's hotspot."

"Yeah, I'll let you suggest that," Ellington said. "Something seems to be bothering him lately and I don't want to be the one to—"

"Stop!"

She nearly screamed it because the thought had come so suddenly. Ellington did as she asked, hitting the brakes and causing the car to jerk a bit in the snow. While the roads were far from covered yet, what had accumulated was making conditions rather slick.

"What is it?" he asked.

"That side road back there…there were tracks."

Ellington backed the car up and came to the side road. It was another of those off-the-beaten path roads like they had seen on State Route 14. This one was located roughly a quarter of a mile from the Ayers farm. There was no gate, just tufts of dead weeds along the side of the road.

Sure enough, there *did* appear to be tracks. They were barely visible in the snow but they were there.

*But the tracks I'm seeing are tracks in the snow. This new snow is covering them up—which means these tracks are surely no older than an hour or two.*

"Think this clunker can get us down there?" Ellington asked.

"I think we can try it."

Ellington turned onto the road and Mackenzie saw at once that it was a very old road. Two thin dirt tracks showed the area where numerous tires had rolled across the ground but that was it. There was no gravel, no easily defined sides to the road—nothing. However, the further down the road they got, the easier it was to see the ghostlike tracks.

Fortunately, the road was not very long. After about half a mile, the road took a hard right turn, in the direction of Ayers's farm. The road stretched out for another two hundred yards or so and then came to a stop in a small field that was mostly filled by a pond.

Ellington parked the car and they stepped out. Mackenzie looked around on the ground but it was mostly hard-packed dirt or dead grass, making it harder to see the tracks. She looked out to the pond and the trees that bordered it on all sides. If Mackenzie had to guess, the pond was about one hundred feet across and one hundred and fifty feet wide from end to end. This, she assumed, wasn't so much a pond as it was what she'd often heard referred to as a *fishing hole.*

She walked toward the water, watching the snow fall onto the surface and then slowly dissolve into the water. As she scanned the banks, she saw another set of tracks, but they made no sense. The tracks they had followed in reappeared right at the edge of the pond. They did not turn away, but continued to go straight…

"Holy shit," Mackenzie said.

She took the final few steps to the edge of the water and looked into it. There was not much murkiness to the water thanks to the still and pristine winter conditions. This made it quite easy for her to see the strange square shape, sitting up at an angle. It was perhaps four feet beneath the water and even through the water and slowly falling snow, she could see that it was beige.

"Ellington, I found the truck."

He came over quickly and let out a nervous chuckle. "Oh my God," he said.

Mackenzie took out her cell phone and called Bateman. The reception was not the best but she heard him well enough when he answered.

"This is Bateman," he answered.

"This is White. We found Missy Hale's truck."

"What? That was quick. Where are you?"

"Down a short dirt road about half a mile away from the Ayers farm. I'm standing at the edge of a pond, looking at the rear end of the truck under the water."

"Wait…half a mile away? Back towards town?"

"Yes. Why?"

There was a pause before Bateman answered rather uneasily. "That's David Ayers's pond."

***

Twenty minutes later, the field in front of the small pond was bustling with activity. Mackenzie and Ellington sat in their rental car with David Ayers, staying out of the cold. Meanwhile, two men had geared up in thermal suits to venture into the pond. They were currently working to hook the truck to a hitch that was attached to the back of a tow truck that had parked at the very edge of the pond. Bateman was speaking to the tow truck driver while Roberts and several other officers stood by, watching.

"This is unreal," Ayers said. He was looking out at the pond as if he might be sick.

"Can I ask why you don't keep your private property blocked off to others?" Mackenzie asked. "We've seen several of these little side roads that are chained off all along the back roads of Bent Creek."

"Because I made the mistake of giving people the benefit of the doubt. Most people in Bent Creek know that they are welcome to come down here and fish whenever they want. I don't mind. Most of the fishing done out here is fathers with their kids and maybe the occasional pair of men that come out to drink and complain about their marriages. I'm happy to offer the space."

"So anyone is allowed to come down here?" Ellington asked. "Do they ever call and ask permission?"

"Some do. But after they call the first time, I always tell them a call isn't necessary."

"So in other words," Mackenzie said, "there's no way to know who came down here this morning."

"That's right."

Mackenzie looked back out to the pond. The men had come out of the water and were stripping out of their gear on the opposite side of the truck. The driver then hit a lever that had the cable start to pull in. There was a groan of protest but then the truck started to slowly reveal itself. It came out of the water sluggishly as the driver pulled the tow truck slowly ahead.

Mackenzie looked to the surrounding forests, now starting to catch the snow. *Whoever drove that truck into the pond had to have left on foot. There are no tracks leaving the field. And if they left on foot, the snow will have covered up their tracks. Another dead end.*

"Thanks for your assistance once again, Mr. Ayers," Mackenzie said. She stepped out of the car and walked over to the tow truck. Bateman and Roberts were already opening the doors to the truck. A thin stream of water cascaded out.

"This is a fucking nightmare," Bateman said. "I won't even lie...I was almost hoping to find a body in here."

"May I?" she asked, walking to the opened door.

"Help yourself."

Mackenzie looked inside the truck, a little overwhelmed by the stagnant smell of pond water that came rushing out toward her. The truck looked relatively clean, albeit soaked. The only thing notable that she spotted was an iPhone that had been washed down onto the floorboard and pinned underneath the gas pedal. She snatched it out and saw that it was remarkably still powered up and working. Its expensive Otterbox case had apparently saved it.

"You have any way to get beyond her password screen?" Bateman asked.

"We can make a call," Mackenzie said. But really, she didn't think it would do any good. Unless the man they were after had called her, she doubted they'd find anything of use on the phone.

Mackenzie checked her watch. It was just after eleven. The day suddenly seemed to be creeping away from them.

*The man was on foot after this,* she reminded herself. *And given that she had a full meeting at the slaughterhouse, that gives a thin window of time. Even if he put the car in the pond fifteen minutes after her meeting, that gives him just a little over two hours to work with. On foot, he'd be slow. But what if he had another vehicle somewhere close by, waiting for him? If he* is *a local, he'd know spots to hide his other car.*

"Sheriff, I think we need to call a lockdown."

"Of the whole town?"

"No. But this guy was on foot when he left here." She then went on to tell him her thoughts, right down to the possibility that he had stowed another vehicle away nearby.

"Well if he *did* have another car, even within a mile of here, he could be out of town by now. I can't lock down the whole town based on a mere *hope*."

It was the first actual resistance she had seen from him but she also knew he had a point. Besides, they didn't even have a single idea of who they were looking for. It would result in a lot of unnecessary stops at the outskirts of town, which would also mean a tired and demoralized police force.

"If you can find me something to go on," Bateman said, "I can maybe work with you. But I can't have officers at every exit out of town without any idea of what they're looking for."

"I understand," Mackenzie said. "How about other properties within walking distance of here? Can we get some people to check for any suspicious activity? Maybe even people who saw this truck going past their house?"

"Yes, we can do that."

The hell of it was that from here, there were no visible footprints other than their own to go by. The fresh snowfall had covered up any that had been left behind.

"And maybe a few officers should scan the edge of the woods for any clear signs of someone having passed through recently," Mackenzie added. "If this guy left here on foot no more than two hours ago—"

"Then any signs are going to be covered up fast by this damned snow," Bateman continued.

Bateman gave her a nod as she headed back for her car. Ellington joined along beside her, giving the water-logged government truck one last glance over his shoulder.

"What's our next move?" he asked.

Maybe it was because she was getting frustrated with the lack of leads or maybe his tone—she wasn't sure. But this time, it *did* sound like he was almost testing her or undermining her. She was sure this was not his intent but it was starting to come across in such a way.

Grasping for straws now, Mackenzie gave the only idea she had left. "Missy Hale was last seen at the slaughterhouse. And since the slaughterhouse seems to be the nexus of this town, I say we go pay a visit to the last person who spoke to her. Maybe we can get a gauge on Missy Hale's mood upon leaving."

"Better than nothing," Ellington said as they got into the car.

He backed the car out as well as he could around the five other vehicles in the field. Mackenzie gave the scene one last look as they headed back down the dirt road toward the blacktop. The snow was coming down a bit harder now, causing Ellington to put the wiper blades on. The increasing snow, she knew, would make things harder on them. With this knowledge, the wiper blades moving back and forth across the glass sounded less like a way to remove the snow and more like the ticking of a very impatient clock.

## CHAPTER TWENTY TWO

"This snow is going to make things a lot harder," Ellington said as they crept closer and closer to the slaughterhouse. The roads were not yet treacherous, but it wouldn't take much longer. "If it's okay with you, I'd like to divide and conquer."

"What are we dividing and conquering?" she asked.

"Well, it's only going to take one person to get information from the slaughterhouse—if there is any to be had. Meanwhile, one of us could check out some of these smaller farms around here that no one has bothered investigating. And I'd like to give it a shot before the damned snow makes it impossible."

"Which farms did you have in mind?" she asked.

"Looking at those maps this morning, there were two that I saw. One isn't too far away from the slaughterhouse."

"That's a good idea," she said.

"Of course it is," he said with a grin. "So why don't I drop you off at the slaughterhouse and pick you up about an hour later? That should give me enough time to check out at least the one closer to the slaughterhouse."

"That could work," she said. Honestly, though, she didn't like the idea of being stranded at the Bent Creek slaughterhouse without a mode of transportation. But she trusted Ellington and his intuition so she said nothing of it.

Ellington drove slowly through the snow. As they made their way through the center of town, they passed two state trucks, one with a plow on the front and the other dumping a generous amount of salt and chemicals on the road, hoping to combat the snowfall before it got any worse. While Mackenzie viewed the slaughterhouse as being the heartbeat of the town, it was, in fact, located at the very edge of the Bent Creek town limits. And despite having to drive all the way across town in snow, they came to the entrance in less than twenty minutes.

Ellington drove her straight to the front door, using a roundabout road that connected the highway to what Mackenzie assumed were loading docks around back. Several other parking lots were scattered here and there, presumably for employees.

Before she closed the door behind her, Mackenzie peered back into the car. Seeing him with a look of determination on his face, plus the almost protective way he looked back at her, brought back a rush of emotion from last night.

"Don't go off being some lone cowboy," she said. "If anything pops up, give me a call."

"I will. Same goes for you. I'll give you a call on my way back."

She closed the door, doing her best to understand the feeling that was urging through her. It wasn't love; she wasn't naïve enough to go that far. But she was certainly developing some sort of feelings for him.

*And you can figure all of that out once this case is wrapped up,* she thought. *For now, keep focused. McGrath wants you back in DC and this snow is going to seriously complicate things.*

She walked up a short yet wide flight of stairs toward the slaughterhouse entrance. Having never visited a slaughterhouse before, she was a bit surprised by the appearance of the place. She had been expecting some worn down factory, something industrial and gray. But the front of the large building looked almost like any professional business she had seen. It was more of the same as she stepped in through the front doors. She found herself in a nicely decorated lobby that served as a waiting area of sorts. A single receptionist sat behind a small glass partition on the far side of the room, speaking on the phone. A closed door sat in the wall directly beside her office.

Mackenzie made her way to the receptionist just as she was finishing her phone call. She looked to Mackenzie with a smile that was obviously rehearsed and all part of the job.

"Hi," Mackenzie said, subtly showing the woman her badge. She spoke quietly, not wanting to draw attention from one of the three people currently sitting in the waiting area. "I'm Agent Mackenzie White with the FBI. I need to speak to whoever had a meeting with Missy Hale of the Department of Agriculture this morning."

The woman's rehearsed pleasant face was wiped away. It was replaced by suspicion and concern. "Of course. Let me page my supervisor and find out who that was."

Mackenzie waited as the receptionist did her job. She wondered how much of Bent Creek's economy came out of this slaughterhouse. She'd heard of small towns that basically thrived only because of lumber yards; she supposed it might be the same for Bent Creek and their slaughterhouse. It would certainly explain the success of a few of the farms in the area.

From the other side of the glass, the receptionist set her phone down. "Come on back," she said, standing up from her chair and opening the door by her closed-off office.

The receptionist led her down a small hallway and didn't even make it to the end of it before a middle-aged man started to approach them from the other end. The man had the same look the receptionist had shown seconds ago. He was clearly worried; the presence of the FBI in a slaughterhouse was surely not sitting well with him.

The receptionist seemed glad to hand Mackenzie off to him. She didn't say a single word as she turned around and headed back to her station.

"Agent White," the middle-aged man said, offering his hand. "I'm Carl Houghton. What can I do for you?"

Even before she started to speak, Carl Houghton led her down the hall and into his office. It was a huge office that showed signs of a man who loved his work. Two large dry erase boards clung to the walls, filled with notes. His desk was well cleaned but also seemed somehow filled with well-organized work. Books, folders, and stacks of paper sat like a wall along the sides.

"You spoke with Missy Hale this morning, correct?" Mackenzie asked as she took a seat in front of his desk.

"I did," Houghton said. He did not sit, opting to stand at the edge of his desk. It was clear that he was concerned. He was apparently not a man who was used to something throwing him off of his usual course.

"Was it a successful meeting?" Mackenzie asked.

"Yes. It always is. She comes by to look in on waste disposal and to have a look at our quarterly numbers, making sure we're not doing *too* well. There's only a certain amount of meat we're allowed to ship out each quarter."

"Are you aware that when she left here, she was scheduled to meet with a farmer in Bent Creek?"

"I knew she had a short morning ahead of her. She revealed that much through small talk."

"And do you think she maybe seemed bothered or nervous?"

"I wouldn't say so," Houghton said. "She was rather happy, I think. She might have been a little upset about snow in the forecast but other than that she seemed normal to me."

"I ask these questions because she never made it to her next meeting," Mackenzie said. "In fact, the truck she was driving was pulled from a local pond less than half an hour ago."

"My God! Are you serious?"

"Yes. Now, as far as we know, she is still alive. She was not in the truck and we have reason to believe that she may be another victim of whoever has been capturing women along the roads here

117

in Bent Creek. So could you *please* think very hard and make sure there was nothing out of the ordinary?"

She could tell that Houghton was doing exactly that. But after about five seconds, he shrugged and shook his head. "I'm sorry, but no…I saw nothing amiss. No red flags, no warning signs, nothing."

"Would you say you know Missy well?"

"Well, it's always been strictly a working relationship. But I see her four times a year and she sometimes even comes to the Christmas party we have. But in terms of her personal life, I don't know much. I know she isn't married, no kids, none of that. She seemed to like her job and always had a laugh to share. Other than that…I'm sorry, but no."

Mackenzie had one other question in mind but was hesitant to even ask it. It was such a shot in the dark that she thought even Carl Houghton might get a glimpse into just how out of her hands this case had become. But she had no other option. She was literally running on fumes here, the case rapidly getting away from her.

"How long have you worked here, Mr. Houghton?"

"It was twenty years as of this past June."

"In that time, have you ever had any employees that were off the range? Anyone that maybe quit over bad blood?"

"There have been a few here and there, yes. But there's never been anything huge. No knock-down arguments that tilted the world or anything. I do remember a case where we had to let an employee go about three years ago. We discovered he was involved in dog fighting. We found it inhumane and, since we go to great lengths to protect the environment and try to be as humane as we can—for a slaughterhouse, anyway—we let him go."

"Did he go peacefully?"

"Yes. He understood. He was quite remorseful about it."

"And what's the turnover rate like here?"

"Pretty good. We offer great hourly pay and the salaries are among the top five of any business of this size in the state."

"I wonder…how hard would it be to get a list of people that have quit of their own accord over the last several years?"

"I can have HR put that together for you," he said. "When would you need it?"

"The sooner the better. And maybe put a bit of urgency on the employee that was fired because of the dog fights."

"Might I ask why?"

She nearly told him, but decided not to. But a thought had suddenly occurred to her, one that she hoped might lead to some sort of breakthrough. *This guy must have known Missy was leaving the slaughterhouse. Either that or he was damned lucky to just* happen *to catch her between meetings. That could mean he knew her schedule. And if he knew her schedule, he's either familiar with the way the slaughterhouse works or has access to the schedules of employees within the Department of Agriculture.*

"We're just taking precautions. This was the last place she was seen, so we can't leave any stone unturned."

*Oh, Ellington would have loved to have heard that,* she thought.

"Well, I'll certainly make sure HR makes it a priority. What would be the best way to get the information to you?"

"Just deliver it to Sheriff Bateman via e-mail," she said. She then got to her feet, realizing that she had another half an hour before Ellington was due to pick her up. "Would you mind if I had a talk with your HR employees to make sure they know what to look for?"

"That's perfectly fine," Houghton said. "Anything we can do to help, just let me know. Come on and I'll take you down to HR."

Mackenzie followed him out of the office, again feeling a huge sense of failure. How had they not uncovered a single solid lead on this guy yet? Doing something as brazen as putting a government vehicle into a pond should turn up *something.*

*Maybe he's getting overly cocky or desperate,* she thought. *Not only did he abduct Missy Hale in broad daylight, but he also dumped a government vehicle in a pond. He's going to keep it up and eventually screw up.*

But what if he didn't? What if he was done with kidnapping and was on to other things now? Mackenzie knew it was a very real possibility and did not like to think of what those *other things* might be.

As Houghton led her back into the building to the HR offices, they passed a large window in the hallway. She looked out and watched the snow continue to fall, turning the world white and making her job harder with each freshly fallen flake.

# CHAPTER TWENTY THREE

Missy Hale had a stubborn streak in her. It was something that her first grade teacher had noticed and set up subsequent parent-teacher conferences. It was likely the very same reason she had never been able to hold a serious relationship for more than eight or nine months. At thirty-five years of age, she recognized the stubborn streak and understood that it was not something to be proud of.

Yet as she sat in the back of what appeared to be a small cattle cart of some kind, it was that stubborn streak that she was relying on. She was pretty sure it was the only reason she was not a blubbering mess right now.

She was scared, she was in pain, but she was also pissed off. There was a huge bump on her forehead, a result of being blasted in the head with what she was pretty sure had been the side of a large carpenter's hammer. She ran her fingers along the knot, wincing not only at the pain but at the sheer size of the damned thing.

*You were a stupid girl today,* she thought. *How did you fall for that?*

She still saw the guy slumped over in his truck. He'd been a good actor for sure, but still…even in a small town like Bent Creek (or, perhaps, *especially* in this kind of town), she knew women had to exercise caution out on those mostly abandoned back roads.

She had no real idea of how long she had been knocked out. She'd opened her eyes roughly ten or fifteen minutes ago. When she'd felt panic sweeping through her head and heart, she stifled it right away. It was much easier than she'd expected and she was pretty sure the immense pain in her head had helped; it had given her something else to focus on.

Since then, she'd allowed herself a few moments of fear but that was it. After that had come and gone, the stubborn streak had kicked in. It told her that not only was she going to be okay, but she was going to get out of here soon.

Wherever *here* was.

She'd had an appointment with David Ayers at 9:00. It was currently 11:05, according to her watch. Surely a phone call had already been made. Probably David Ayers to her supervisor and then, if she was lucky, her supervisor to her cell phone. And although her phone had been left in her truck, she was pretty sure alarms were being raised due to her not answering. She didn't know how long it would take for the police to get involved, but she figured her chances of getting out of this were pretty good.

Of course, she had no idea what *this* was. The man she'd stopped to assist had attacked her and was currently holding her in some type of container. From the inside, she was pretty sure it was one of the industrial containers that livestock were often carried around in. And if that was the case, she was pretty sure she would not be able to get out by herself.

She saw nothing more than some dirt, old hay fragments, and a wooden wall in front of her. That, plus the musty smell and the faint scent of some sort of manure, made her think she was in a barn. She was being held in a cattle container in a barn somewhere around Bent Creek. She thought of David Ayers but knew there was no way he would be capable of such a thing.

Finally, using her stubbornness to summon up some courage, Missy walked to the front of the container. She had to hunch over, bent almost in half to advance forward. There, she found that there appeared to be a layer of chicken wire that had been fastened across the front of the container between the lip of the container and the actual gate. With this second layer of security, she was pretty sure there was no way to escape.

That meant she had two options: sit idly by, hoping the guy that captured her wouldn't kill her soon, or screaming for the guy and hoping to have some sort of rational conversation with him. Neither option appealed to her, but she'd be damned if she'd just sit still and wait for her fate to be decided for her.

She banged at the chicken wire and started to yell. She was only able to let out a single yet powerful, *"HELLO!"* before the pain in her head erupted like a volcano in the center of her skull.

She stumbled back from the pain and was sure she was going to throw up. She was instantly hazy, dizzy, and nauseous. It also felt like someone was driving a spike into her forehead.

*This asshole really did a number on me,* she thought. And with that realization, the stubborn and fighting side of her started to shrink a bit.

Seconds later, she heard a loud clanging noise and the sound of what she thought were huge hinges. *Barn doors opening,* she thought.

The hell of it was, she knew almost everyone that owned a farm in Bent Creek. There were a few smaller ones that she had never visited but that was because they weren't large enough to warrant the interest or resources of the Department of Agriculture.

She heard footsteps coming forward and then a shadow fell across the chicken wire as a man stood in front of the container. He dropped down to his haunches and peered in at her. Looking at him through the chicken wire, Missy was pretty sure she had never seen this man before.

"Scream like that again," the man said, "and I'll knock your teeth out."

"Please," she said. "What do you want? Just tell me…let me know and we can put this behind us, right?'

The man laughed at her, a maniacal laugh that made Missy wonder if he was crazy. He had a thoughtful look on his face and then looked to the left, away from the container. "One minute," he said. "Keep your mouth shut."

Something in his eyes made Missy quite afraid of him, so she figured she'd do as he said for now. She remained quiet, cowering in the back of the container as the man walked away from the container and to somewhere deeper within the barn.

He came back a few seconds later with a gnarled strip of burlap in one hand and a small machete in the other. He leered at her through the barred gate and the chicken wire, tapping menacingly on the wire with the machete.

"Stay right there at the back and put your hands on the floor. You try to run or hit me, I'll hack away at you. Understand?"

She fought not to beg and plead, obeying his orders. She gave a weak little nod. Her head was still pounding, making the entire scene all the more surreal.

He unlatched the bars of the gate and drew them open. He then set about unfastening the chicken wire. She supposed he had screwed some type of hinges onto them or maybe even just simple wood planks to keep the wire stationary. He had it all removed in less than ten seconds and then he was hunching down to join her within the container.

He slid the machete along the side of the container, smiling a young boy's smile that made the harshness of his eyes look evil and damn near the stuff of lunatics. She cringed and pressed herself back against the wall of the container.

"I'm not going to hurt you," he said. "I never will if you don't give me a reason to. For right now, I'm just going to put this burlap round your mouth. You keep screaming and someone might discover our little secret. Understand? So you don't fight and this will be over very soon."

Maybe she was the lunatic. She wanted to believe him—she hoped the words he was saying were true, daring to put some sort of hope into them.

He slunk through the container in a way that was almost like a morbid dance, still dragging the machete. When he reached her, he was not subtle at all. He reached out and caressed the side of her face. He then placed the strip of burlap across her mouth. He wrapped it tight around her face twice, tying it behind her head. With what was left over, he tore it away and bound her hands. As he looped the burlap around her wrists, he looked her in the eyes and smiled.

"This won't stay on your hands," he said. "When I come to you and we make love, I'll release your hands. I'm not a total barbarian." He then gave her an unnerving wink, leaned forward, and kissed her on the neck.

She whimpered against it and hit her head on the back of the container. Another flare of pain passed through her just as he backed away. "It won't be long," he said. "Soon enough, we're all going to be happy together. You'll see. I've had my eye on you for a while, Missy. You hold a special place among the rest."

*My God, he's crazy,* Missy thought. *I don't know if that helps me in this case or not and I...oh God, oh God...*

The slamming of the gate jarred the thought from her mind. She was left simply trembling in the back of the metal box, feeling that determined and stubborn part of her crumble away bit by bit.

# CHAPTER TWENTY FOUR

No more than ten minutes had passed since he had bound and gagged Missy Hale when Harry Givens saw the car come slowly bouncing up his driveway. He was in his side yard, running his wood splitter. So much of his concentration had been on the women lately and he'd let his woodpile get low. And now that it was snowing, he figured he'd best get a good pile stoked up and inside his cellar before all of his firewood got wet.

But now that Harry saw the car coming up his driveway, keeping a dry supply of wood was the least of his concerns. Seeing an unfamiliar car so soon after gagging Missy—it didn't feel right.

*You were stupid to ditch that truck like that,* he thought to himself. *The snow has probably covered your tracks by now, but it sure as hell wasn't about to cover up a government truck.*

Deep down, he'd known this. He'd simply been counting on no one finding the truck until after the snow had fallen…hell, probably not for a week or two after that. And by then, he'd be long gone.

But here was this car he'd never seen before. It sure wasn't a cop car, not even one of the broken down models Bateman and his boys drove around town. Still, it did not sit well with Harry—especially not when it parked and a man in a suit stepped out.

The suited man spotted him in the side yard just as he placed another length of wood on the splitter. Acting as if the presence of the suited man didn't bother him, Harry pulled the crank back, sending the motorized wedge forward, trapping the piece of wood between the wedge and the back post of the splitter. The wood creaked and then burst in half, split evenly down the center. He then retracted the wedge by pulling the crank back toward him and readying the splitter for another piece. By the time the splitter was ready for the next piece of wood, the suited man was about twenty feet away.

He smiled at the suited man and killed the engine on the splitter. As he sized the suited man up, Harry was also very aware of the axe that sat about five feet to his right, propped against a knotted length of maple.

"Sorry to bother you," the suited man said, taking a few steps closer. He pulled something out of the inside pocket of his suit jacket and showed it to him. It was an FBI badge.

*Shit,* he thought. And for the first time since he had taken his first girl, he started to panic.

"I'm Agent Ellington with the FBI," the suited man said. "I was hoping you might have a few minutes to talk."

"A few," he said, doing everything he could not to seem angry. "But I'd really like to get this all split up before the snow comes down even harder."

"I can appreciate that," Ellington said. "I'll make it as quick as I can then. I'm in town looking into a string of recent disappearances."

"Yeah, that's terrible," he said. "I heard about the author. Something Manning, I think."

"Yes, that's right. And honestly, we're just checking around the farms for any information we can find. Any place off of the road is being checked out."

"Well, that's damn near any house when you live somewhere like Bent Creek," Harry said. "What exactly do you need from me?"

"Nothing, really. Just some basic information. For starters, what kind of farm do you run here?"

Harry chuckled and gave an exaggerated sigh. "Nothing much these days, to tell you the truth. I tried pigs, but don't have the patience. So I don't even call it a farm anymore. I have some success with corn and tomatoes in the summer, but that's about it."

Agent Ellington looked to the back of the property, across his backyard and toward the two sheds. "What's in those?" he asked.

"Well, the one on the right is mostly filled with barn wood. There's a few old lawn mowers and a motorcycle I planned on rebuilding but never got around to. The other, I use for a bunch of different things. Storing crops in the spring and summer, a little work space for engine repair, storage…everything, really. You're welcome to go have a look."

As Agent Ellington thought this over, Harry once again felt the axe, just within reach. If Ellington *did* decide to snoop around, Harry figured he'd have to use it. He'd already put a government truck in a pond today…maybe offing a government agent with an axe to the forehead would be the icing on the cake for the morning.

"Thanks," Ellington said. And, to Harry's horror, he started walking toward the barns. He was walking toward the one on the right, the one Harry had come out of fifteen minutes ago. Fortunately, the footprints he'd made coming in and out of them were mostly covered by the snow.

Wanting to seem as normal as possible and to cover up any bravery Missy Hale might be capable of, he cranked the splitter back to life. Ellington cast him an annoyed look but carried on with his business.

*Grab the axe,* Harry told himself. *Kill him. Do it now.*

Harry's heart started to hammer hard in his chest. An excitement like the one he got when he had taken the women surged through him. He watched the FBI agent walk toward the shed, the snow coming down in fat flakes around him.

Slowly, Harry reached out for the axe.

*\*\*\**

For a strange reason she had not understood, Missy had calmed down a bit when she'd heard the sound of a small engine cranking to life. This had happened almost immediately after her captor had left her gagged and bound in the container. She supposed the sound calmed her because it meant he was otherwise occupied. After the engine noise, she'd also heard the pleasant sound of wood splintering, popping, and clattering into a pile. He was apparently splitting wood, using one of those engine-driven wood splitters.

The taste of burlap filled her mouth and the loops around her wrists were a little too tight. She realized now that her only hope was that the police would come, alerted by a string of phone calls that would have resulted from missing her meeting with David Ayers.

As her frazzled mind tried to imagine what this scene might look like as it played out—her boss being called and then, in turn, calling to start a search for her—she heard the engine on the wood splitter come to a stop. He'd apparently not needed much wood, as the engine had only been running for about ten minutes or so.

Her fear was that he'd come back to her. He'd been talking crazy, but she'd gathered a few things. First, she was pretty sure he had captured more than one woman. Second, he planned on raping her, although he had referred to it as *making love.*

After a few moments, she was pretty sure he was not coming back. Not right away. She heard a brief silence and then a muted conversation. She could hear the words but they seemed thin and far away. It made her again wonder where she was being held. Outside of her cattle crate, she was pretty sure she was inside of a barn or shed of some sort. But beyond that, she had no idea.

She listened closely to the conversation, missing a few words here and there but catching enough to make her heart surge with hope.

*"Sorry to bother you,"* someone said. She was pretty sure this was not the voice of the man that she had seen fifteen or twenty minutes ago. This was confirmed with his next statement: *"I'm*

*Agent Ellington with the FBI. I was hoping you might have a few minutes to talk."*

"*A few,*" someone else responded and this *was* her captor.

*The FBI,* she thought as they continued to speak somewhere nearby. *I can try screaming through this thing. He might hear me.*

She started trying to scream but the burlap against her mouth made it hard. It came out in a strangled sort of wail. As she gathered up her breath, she heard more of their conversation. "*...in town looking into a string of recent disappearances."*

She tried screaming again and realized that it just wasn't going to work with the gag on her mouth. She backed against the back of the container and tried moving her head up and down, hoping to loosen the knot he had tied. She also tried rubbing her wrists together, hoping to loosen the bind around her wrists, but that only seemed to make things worse. The asshole sure seemed to know his way around a knot.

She slid on her knees to the front of the container and placed her back against the chicken wire. She again bobbed her head up and down, hoping the burlap would catch on the knot. It did a few times but the burlap always slipped off, doing nothing to weaken the gag around her mouth.

As she gathered breath for another scream, she heard even more of the conversation—a piece that again filled her with a desperate hope. It was her captor talking this time. "*...work space for engine repair, storage...everything, really. You're welcome to go have a look."*

And then, moments later, she heard footsteps. From the sound they made as they approached the shed, she figured the snow had really started to come down now. She could hear the light crunching of snow under the agent's shoes.

But then the wood splitter fired up again. It was no longer calming to her, but menacing. She could not hear anything over it and had no clue of how things were playing out.

She tried screaming again but all it did was rattle her head and make her throat feel raw. She then tried kicking at the container but the sound it made was dense and hollow. She seriously doubted that the sound would reach any ears outside of the barn she was currently in. Still, she kicked and kicked until jolts of what felt like electricity raced up from her feet into her knees.

She collected her wits and sat there for a moment. *Just let the agent do his job,* she thought. *He'll open the barn door and find the container and—*

But something about that felt wrong. Why would her captor willingly let the agent into the barn? The only thing she could figure was it was some type of a set-up. She found herself frozen then, waiting for the engine on the wood splitter to stop one more time.

Instead, the engine noise remained and, over it, she heard the agent's voice. He spoke in a near-shout and seemed impossibly close.

*"It's locked!"* he yelled.

A few moments passed and then the engine died again. She could barely hear her captor and in her heart she hated him for the stellar acting job he was doing. She looked through the slats in the container and her heart again felt like it was doing a flip. She could actually *see* the agent; she saw his shoulder and the side of his face through a warped crack in the barn door.

"Ah shit, I forgot," her captor said. When he continued, he sounded annoyed but also a little eager to please. "Hold on. I have to run inside and get the key."

Two seconds passed—Missy knew it was two seconds because she was literally counting every moment now that rescue was so close—before she heard another noise. It was the ringing of a cell phone, coming from the agent.

"This is Ellington," the agent said. She then listened to his side of the conversation. "Yeah? Okay, that makes sense. Damn. Yeah, I'll be there as soon as I can."

She then heard the lock clatter back to the door. "Forget about it," the FBI agent said. "It's okay. Just…let me get your name and number in case there are any more questions."

Against the burlap, Missy cried out. *"No!"* She heard it perfectly in her head but knew that it had gone unheard by anyone else. She then tried screaming one more time but by the time it was out, she was crying instead. She stamped her feet hard against the floor and then the wall of the container but got only a flaring pain in her ankles as a reward.

She heard the agent's footfalls walking away, lightly crunching in the snow. She let out one final guttural roar, this one so fierce that her head seemed to vibrate with it. But even then she still knew that it would not be loud enough.

She wept, nearly choking on her sobs with the gag pulled so tightly over her mouth. When the small engine of the wood splitter started back up, Missy curled herself into a ball and lost herself. Her stubborn streak was gone. There was no more fight in her. She felt herself giving up and in a strange way, it made everything a little easier to manage.

## CHAPTER TWENTY FIVE

Mackenzie sat in the lobby for five minutes before Ellington called her. It was just 12:05 when she got into the car. The snow had found a comfortable pace, now falling steadily. While the snowfall was not at snowstorm proportions, it had managed to cover the yards they passed in a thin blanket of white. She figured they had about another three hours of being able to travel on the roads, so she wanted to make the best use of that time.

They both briefly shared their lack of results. Mackenzie told him about the ex-employee that had been involved in dog fighting and speculated that tons of things went down in Bent Creek that were both illegal and required animal transport crates. Ellington told her about heading out to the farm, finding nothing, and then being called to the station to speak with Earl Temper about the location of pine groves—a thirty-minute exercise that had amounted to nothing.

Mackenzie frowned. She felt like an ant trying to scale a mountain. This day was taking its toll on both of them and the snow wasn't helping.

"Hear me out on something," Mackenzie said as they came to the exit of the slaughterhouse parking lot.

"Okay," Ellington said. "I'm willing to hear *any* ideas right about now."

"I keep thinking of Delores Manning. I still say she's our best bet for finding this guy. Of course, yesterday, we caught her straight out of her traumatic experience. The brain processes things in a strange way when trauma is involved, would you agree?"

"Yes, from what I understand."

"So, I'd like to go see her again before these roads become too hazardous."

"Like right now?"

"Yes. But that's not it. Even if she still has problems coming up with information, I can almost guarantee you there's bits of information—small details, really—right there at the edge of her memory. And if she's recovered well enough, I think we can get her to remember them."

"How?"

"With the help of a hypnotist."

Ellington gave her a look that she did not understand at first. But when the traces of a smiled touched the corners of his mouth, she understood that he was trying to decide if she was being serious or not. "Oh…" he said. "You're serious."

"Yes. I've seen it work on a woman with a history of abuse in the past. And I've read countless studies about the effectiveness of it."

"I've probably read all those same studies," he said. "But I really don't know if driving back to Cedar Rapids in this shitty weather is worth delving into some New Age practices for—"

"There's nothing New Age about it," she said. "It's a legitimate yet underappreciated psychological tool. And because these things happened to Delores so recently, I think we stand a very good chance of getting some answers."

"But you do know that any details gathered form hypnosis aren't admissible in court, right?"

"I know that," Mackenzie said. "But we're not working on a trial here…we're trying to find three abducted women."

Ellington sighed as he looked back out to the snow. "Well, it's more productive than sitting here in Bent Creek, waiting for enough snow to make a snowman. You got a hypnotist in your back pocket?"

"No," she said. "I'm going to call the Omaha branch and see if I can get Thorsson or Heideman to find one—hopefully somewhere in Des Moines or Cedar Rapids."

"Hopefully the snow won't make it an impossibility."

Mackenzie had been thinking the exact same thing. Still, she got on her phone and called up Thorsson as Ellington made a right turn and started down the increasingly snowy roads. As the phone rang in her ear, Mackenzie watched the snow continue to fall and found it a little hypnotizing. The irony of this, though, was a little eerie rather than funny.

\*\*\*

It took less than twenty minutes for Agent Thorsson to call her back. By that time, she and Ellington had barely made it out of Bent Creek, slowed by the snow.

"Well, Agent White," Thorsson said, "I'll give you this: it appears that you have a tremendous amount of luck on your side."

"How so?"

"There's a licensed professional counselor in Cedar Rapids that also works part time as a teacher at a community college. It also happens that she also serves as a consultant and sometimes-hypnotist for psychiatrists in the area. As if that wasn't lucky enough for you, her office is located about four miles away from the hospital."

"Were you able to get in touch with her?" Mackenzie asked.

"Yes. We caught her just before she was leaving her office. She was leaving early because of the snow—snow we aren't getting here in Nebraska, by the way. When we told her what you would need her for, she seemed eager to help. She'll be in the waiting area when you guys get there."

"Thanks, Thorsson."

She ended the call and looked out onto the roads. Plows had come through and salt had been dumped, but the snow was winning the fight on the roads leading out of Bent Creek. Fortunately, when Ellington turned onto the four-lane road that would lead them into Cedar Rapids, the road conditions were much better. The plows had been much more thorough here and it looked as if the roads had been treated with chemical the night before, not *during* the snowfall as had been the case in Bent Creek.

Still, they passed two minor accidents as well as more state trucks spraying down more chemicals. Mackenzie checked the forecast on her phone and saw that the area was due to get around three inches of snow before it all finally passed by later in the evening.

"So," Ellington said, out of the blue, "you still not want to talk about last night?"

The truth of the matter was that she did. But she knew that there was no way it would help the situation they were currently in. Also, it would make her feel far too vulnerable. The scene of their first encounter together in Nebraska was still too easy to recall. She'd offered herself to him and found that he was married. And then last night, while it had not been quite as brutal (it had, in fact, been quite nice up until the end), she still saw it as rejection.

"There's nothing to talk about," she said. "Especially right now."

"But...well, no hard feelings, right?"

She did her best to seem comical when she replied, "Don't flatter yourself."

He gave her a smile and left it at that. The car then fell into small talk about the case for a while. Mackenzie also called the hospital and requested an update on Delores Manning. She was told that Delores was doing much better today and should be discharged by tomorrow morning. Shortly after she received this good news, they arrived at the hospital. The entire trip had taken about twenty minutes longer than they had hoped, due to the roads. They quickly entered the hospital's central waiting area, not wanting to make the hypnotist wait very long.

They found her sitting in a chair, idly watching C-SPAN on a TV that was mounted to the wall. When she saw them enter, she stood up and greeted them. Mackenzie was surprised by how young the woman seemed. She was maybe thirty and quite pretty. She was dressed in a baggy yet dressy sweater and a pair of jeans. Mackenzie wasn't sure what she had been expecting out of a hypnotist, but this wasn't it.

"I'm Agent White and this is Agent Ellington," Mackenzie said. "Thank you so much for meeting with us."

"Of course. I'm Margo Redman. Did you have any questions for me?"

"Not really. I suppose I'm just a bit cautious about how the doctors might respond to the approach."

"If the patient is coherent and has passed basic cognitive tests, I don't see where we'd get any push-back."

Confident in Margo's response, Mackenzie started for the elevators with Margo and Ellington in tow. When they arrived on the third floor and headed for Delores's room, Mackenzie noticed right away that the police guards were no longer posted at her door. She did, however, see the same doctor who had greeted them the day before. He gave them an inquisitive look and Mackenzie assumed the best thing to do would be to include him on what she had planned.

"How is Ms. Manning?" Mackenzie asked.

"She's doing fine," he said. "The EKG showed no trauma and very little swelling. Still, there's the slight hemorrhage and concussion to consider."

"Would you mind if we spoke to her again?" Mackenzie asked.

"I'd be fine with that. But again, if she shows any signs of distress or panic, I'd much rather you stop."

Mackenzie waited for him to add the fact that he'd like to accompany them again as he had done yesterday but he did not. Apparently he either thought Delores was in much better shape or he now trusted Mackenzie and Ellington a bit more.

"Thanks, Doctor," Mackenzie said. She then tapped on the door and opened it, stepping inside.

Delores gave Mackenzie a sleepy-looking nod of acknowledgment as she entered. She also gave a weak smile—a good sign as far as Mackenzie was concerned.

"How are you, Delores?" she asked.

"Much better," she said. "And because my family basically sucks, you're the first visitor I've had all day."

"I'm glad to hear you're doing better. I just spoke with your doctor and he gave me permission to speak with you again if you're up to it."

"That's fine with me," Delores said. "But to be honest…I've tried thinking about what happened. Fragments of it come to me…but there's nothing solid. It's actually pretty frustrating."

"I understand that," Mackenzie said. "That's why I've brought along Margo Redman," she said, stepping aside and letting Margo take the primary spot by the bedside. "I think she might be able to help you to remember."

"Great," Delores said. "But how, exactly?"

"I'd like your permission to hypnotize you," Mackenzie said.

"What?" Delores said, clearly not a fan of the idea. "Does that nonsense even work? I researched it for one of my books and it seemed like a load of crap."

"That's an unfortunate stereotype," Margo said. Her voice was calm and soothing. Mackenzie thought she'd likely had this conversation before. "But there *is* clinical research to back up the effectiveness of it. And I would not be putting you very far under. Being that the events occurred very recently and that you can *almost* see them, I don't think I'll have to do anything very involved at all."

Delores thought it over and shook her head slowly. "I don't know," she said. "Is it safe with what happened to my head? I honestly don't even know what a mild subarachnoid hemorrhage is, but I know it *sounds* bad."

"Honestly," Margo said, "if I had to do something very major and involved, I would probably not be comfortable. But this will be a very basic session. In fact, some studies have shown that slight hypnotic suggestion can actually work to help subdue pain. It's a great tool for rehabilitative suggestion."

"I understand the hesitancy," Mackenzie said. "But…another woman has been taken. This makes three he has taken—four if we include you. And with the snow outside, our job is getting harder. If we can hypnotize you and even get the *smallest* little clue of where this guy is or *who* he is, it could make a world of difference."

Delores looked to the window where snowflakes fell majestically on the other side. Mackenzie couldn't be sure, but she thought she caught a hint of anger in her expression—at them or at the man that had captured her, she had no idea.

"Okay," she said. "Let's do it."

133

Margo pulled up the visitor chair next to the bed and gave the most comforting smile she could muster. "It'll be easy," she said. "Please...I know you don't know me, but trust me. I'll take every precaution I can."

She was speaking in such a somber tone that Mackenzie wondered if she was actually trying to start the hypnosis process without anyone knowing it.

Delores looked a little nervous but relaxed back against the pillows behind her.

"Are you comfortable?" Margo asked.

"Yeah, I guess."

Okay," Margo said. "I need you to just listen to my voice. Listen closely to each word and as you get accustomed to my voice, I want you to slowly close your eyes."

Mackenzie watched as Delores did just that. The hesitancy she'd shown before seemed to melt away within seconds. Her eyes closed slowly, like veils to cover the secrets behind them. Mackenzie and Ellington watched as Margo went on, taking Delores further under to where, hopefully, she'd be able to find those secrets and offer them up.

# CHAPTER TWENTY SIX

Mackenzie found the process of hypnosis fascinating and was in a mild sort of awe as Margo skillfully took Delores down a few steps into her subconscious. She watched Margo's concentration laced into each word and Delores's reaction. She also looked over to Ellington and saw that he, despite his skepticism, was also quite interested.

"Okay, Delores, you're doing great," Margo said. "You should feel quite light now, almost weightless. Do you feel that?"

"Yes," Delores said, sounding like she was very close to a nap.

"I want you to think about a place you find peace," she said. "A place that is special to you…somewhere you feel safe. Can you bring that place to mind?"

"Yes. I'm there."

"Where are you? Tell me some details."

"The first writing space I ever had," she said. "Straight out of college, in my first apartment. It's a little desk, a clunky old Dell laptop on it. The window looks out into the back lot of a bakery. God, I loved that apartment. That writing space…"

"Good, good," Margo said. "I want you to stay there and hang out. And I want you to really latch on to that memory. You're safe there, Margo. But now I'm going to step back and Agent White is going to ask you some questions. I want you to answer them as best as you can but all the while, I want you to stay in that apartment. Do you understand?"

With a smile, her eyes still closed and very clearly at peace, Delores said, "I understand."

Margo stood up from the chair and offered it to Mackenzie. Before she took her seat, Margo spoke quietly into her ear. "Keep your voice soft, quiet, and level. You can't show frustration or concern."

Mackenzie nodded and took the seat. She composed herself, took a calming breath, and resumed the session from where Margo had left off.

"Hi, Delores. This is Agent Mackenzie White. Are you still sitting in your first apartment?"

"Yeah. Looking at that old laptop. I wrote my first book on it."

"That's great, Delores. But for right now, I need you to think about the last time you were in Bent Creek, Iowa. Can you do that for me? Can you tell me why you were there?"

She thought for a moment and then nodded slowly. With her eyes still closed, it was a nearly funny gesture. "I was coming from a book signing in Cedar Rapids. I wasn't looking forward to it, but I was going to see my mother. But I never made it to her trailer. I ran over something in the road, I guess. The tires blew out. But it wasn't long before a man pulled up to help. But...he—"

She paused here. She did not look upset yet, but it was clear she did not want to talk about it. Mackenzie looked back at Margo. Margo mouthed the words *Skip ahead*.

"Never mind the man for now, Delores. I need you to try to remember the things you saw when you were off the road. After that man took you...what can you tell me about where you were or what happened to you?"

"I was...in a box. Like a container. Maybe one of those things they move farm animals around in. Not quite big enough to stand up in. Just a few rectangular slats at the front. He shoved a water bottle through there so I could drink."

"Do you know where the container was?" Mackenzie asked.

"In a shed or barn, maybe. Couldn't see much through those slats."

"Did you smell or hear anything?"

"I don't know...I don't...well, yeah. There was this weird sort of whining sound. I thought it might be animals of some kind but...I don't know. It's a sound I know. A sound I've heard before but I don't know. I can't place it."

Mackenzie looked back to Margo and Ellington. Margo was nodding her approval while Ellington was typing notes into his iPhone.

"Okay, Delores. That's okay. Now I need you to think about escaping. When you got out, what did you see? From the time you made it out of that container to the moment you saw the train...what did you see?"

"I saw *him*," she said. "I told him I had to pee. And I really did. He said he'd let me out but when I was done peeing, he was going to rape me. He told me that. But I kicked him in the nuts...attacked him. I got away."

"Did you see what he looked like?" Mackenzie asked.

"Sort of, but it's...like seeing clouds. Denim clouds. A denim shirt, maybe. Too worried about getting out of there. The barn...outside of the barn, there was a small backyard. Trees everywhere. There were more barns. Two...maybe one. And I heard someone screaming for help. Another woman in another shed. I went back for her...but...I was too scared. Couldn't reach her."

She paused here and showed real emotion for the first time. "Oh my God, I should have helped. I should have—"

Mackenzie was dimly aware of her cell phone buzzing in her pocket as someone called her. She ignored it, hoping to finish up with Delores first.

"That's okay, Delores. What else do you see?"

"Nothing. Just trees. I'm running fast. He's behind me somewhere. I don't…I don't see anything. Just the yard, the sheds. I barely see the back of a house…"

"Is that all?" Mackenzie asked.

Delores was shifting in the bed now. The smile that had been on her face three minutes ago was gone now. It had been replaced by a grim frown. Her head ticked left to right, as if she were watching the woods pass by in her mind's eye while she escaped.

Mackenzie felt a hand on her shoulder. She turned around and saw that Margo had quietly come up behind her. She shook her head as politely as she could and then slashed a finger over her throat. *Stop,* she seemed to be saying. *We're done.*

Mackenzie wanted to argue but kept Delores's health in mind. Frustrated, she stood up from the chair and allowed Margo to sit back down. As she did, Mackenzie heard Ellington's phone vibrating from his interior coat pocket.

*Thirty seconds behind mine,* she thought. *It's either McGrath trying to get us back home ASAP before the snow makes it impossible or there's been a break on Bateman's end in Bent Creek.*

Mackenzie nodded to Ellington, signaling him to answer the call. He withdrew his phone and stepped out into the hallway, closing the door quietly behind him. Mackenzie turned back to the hospital bed, where Margo was easing Delores down and bringing her out of the session.

"Okay, Delores, I need you to step away from that forest and forget the man behind you. I want you to stop running, stand still, and look. I need you to realize that you are not there. You are still sitting in your old apartment. See the window and the bakery's back lot? Do you see it? Do you see the old Dell laptop?"

Slowly, Delores settled down and resumed her relaxed position against the pillows. Her breathing was a little labored, but she seemed to be okay. Margo continued on, her voice still calm and soothing.

"Great job, Delores. You're there, aren't you? In that old apartment."

"Yes," Delores said, clearly relieved.

"Good. Now, I want you to continue listening to my voice. I'm going to count backwards from three and you're going to open your eyes. Do you remember where you are?"

"Hospital."

"That's right. So be ready for that and remember where you are as I count down. Three…you're opening your eyes, Delores. Two, coming up towards my voice, like waking up, and *three*."

It amazed Mackenzie how easy it had seemed. On *three,* Delores's eyes opened slowly. She looked around the room as if in a daze until her eyes landed on Mackenzie and Margo. She gave them a shaky smile and chuckled.

"That was…well, that was odd," she said.

"But you did great," Margo said.

"Did any of that help?" Delores asked.

Mackenzie didn't want to show her disappointment in the lack of answers so she gave a generic reply. "Every little bit helps. Thanks so much for doing this. I already left my number with you yesterday…so if you think of anything else, *please* contact me right away."

"There's a good chance that may happen," Margo said. "Once the memories have been breached, they tend to come back naturally. Sometimes with surprising speed. That includes additional memories that did not surface during hypnosis."

Mackenzie was going to ask one more question, hoping she could get some details on the man that took her. But before she got the chance to ask, Ellington came back into the room. He looked hurried and a little excited.

"Agent White, can I see you in the hallway for a moment?"

She stepped out into the hallway, hoping he had good news. "Is this about the call I ignored while we were in there?"

"Yes. Carl Houghton called the Bent Creek PD. They're just about done with that employee search you requested at the slaughterhouse. Turns out there were a few details about a former employee that he didn't remember. Apparently he had mentioned something to you about an employee that was fired when it was discovered he was holding dogs for dog fights."

"Yes, I remember that."

"Well, that guy's name is Ed Fowley. When Bateman saw the name, it raised some alarms. So he looked back through Bent Creek records and discovered something interesting. In 2011, Fowley was involved in a domestic dispute call. He and his wife got into an argument and he locked her in a cage as a sort of mean-spirited joke. Not just any cage, mind you—a cattle cage that he had once hidden puppies and their mothers in."

"A stretch, but worth checking out, I guess," Mackenzie said.

"Oh…it gets better. Before Fowley and *that* wife eventually divorced, he had troubles with his first wife. They divorced after about a year because she caught him sleeping around. And it just so happens that his mistress was Crystal Hall."

"That sounds like a lead," Mackenzie said.

"Hell yeah, it does," Ellington said. "Bateman is getting a crew ready as we speak. He says he'll wait on us and go in after five, when Fowley will likely be home from work."

"Well then, let's hope the roads are still passable," Mackenzie said.

They hurried down the hall, pushed by the excitement of their first true lead since arriving in Bent Creek. Outside, the snow was dying off but it had done its damage. No amount of plowing or road salt would make the roads completely clear, so they'd have to take things slow and steady…which was easier said than done, knowing that a promising lead was waiting for them elsewhere in the slush and cold.

## CHAPTER TWENTY SEVEN

At 5:37 that afternoon, Mackenzie and Ellington drove behind Sheriff Bateman and Deputy Wickline. Behind Mackenzie and Ellington was a car with two other officers, one of whom was Roberts. The three cars drove almost casually down Bent Creek's main stretch of road and then turned off into a small unmarked road named Skinner's Reach Road. The state trucks had not touched this road; however, there was evidence that a Good Samaritan had been down it with some type of small plow.

Still, Skinner's Reach Road was a hazardous mess. Now that the darkness of a cold winter evening had fallen, wrapping up the day, the snow seemed more treacherous. Even creeping along at twenty miles per hour, Mackenzie could feel the tires sliding a bit on the slick pavement. The snow had stopped falling but it was bitterly cold outside, not making conditions any better.

About a mile down Skinner's Reach Road, Bateman cut on his flashers ahead of them. This, he had told Mackenzie, was their sign that they were less than half a mile from Ed Fowley's residence. The flashers pierced the darkness and seemed to pull them forward.

A few minutes later, Bateman turned off onto a gravel driveway. The small house could be seen from the road, a faint glow spilling out through one of the windows along the front. On the snowed-over gravel, Bateman sped ahead. Ellington increased their speed, too, the tires of the rental car spinning a bit before gaining traction.

With his lights still swirling, Bateman and Wickline got out of the car. Mackenzie and Ellington followed him. As per the plan they had come up with at the station, Roberts and the other officer remained in their car. Walking in a neat single file line through the snow-covered yard, Bateman seemed to begrudgingly allow Mackenzie and Ellington to take the lead. As they stepped up on the small porch, the front door opened quickly…so quickly that Mackenzie caught herself going for her gun. When she saw that the man standing in front of her was thin as a rail and clearly unarmed, she relaxed a bit.

"Sheriff Bateman," the man, presumably Ed Fowley, said. "Lights are just a-flashing out there. Everything okay?"

"I don't know, Ed," Bateman said from behind Mackenzie. "I sure hope so."

Mackenzie then flashed her badge, as did Ellington. "Agents White and Ellington, with the FBI," Mackenzie said. "We'd like to ask you some questions."

The alarm in Fowley's eyes was suddenly very fierce. He did his best to wrangle it in, but Mackenzie saw it quite easily. More than that, he saw that she had noticed it. He took a step back, doing everything he could to remain calm.

"Something wrong, Mr. Fowley?"

"What kinds of questions?" he asked.

"It's rather cold out here," Ellington said. "You think we could maybe come in and have a word?"

Mackenzie could almost smell the panic coming off of him. Still, he gave a nod, a strangled "Yeah," and reluctantly invited them in.

Or so it seemed.

The moment Mackenzie stepped inside the doorway, Fowley wheeled around in a hard arc, drawing up his elbow. It caught her by surprise but she was able to bring her hand up to block it. More than that, she caught his arm and twisted it in a downward pull while also using it as a lever of sorts. She slammed him into the wall just as he let out a shout.

"Backup plan! NOW!" Fowley called out.

"Shit," Ellington said. He went running into the house, drawing his weapon as Mackenzie wrestled Fowley to the floor. He tried fighting against her but a solidly placed knee into his ribs took it out of him.

Bateman was suddenly at her side, yanking a set of handcuffs from his belt. "I'll handle him," he said. "You go catch up with Ellington."

Mackenzie gave Fowley one last knee to the ribs, out of anger more than anything else, and then took off in the direction Ellington had gone. She drew her sidearm and strafed through the living room and into the adjoining hall. She saw Ellington a few steps ahead of her, his gun aimed forward into a room near the back of the hall.

Just as she saw him, a young-looking male came barreling out of the room, hunched over. He held a baseball bat in his hands, swinging it upward as they came out. Ellington lowered his gun but was struck before he could give a warning. The bat took him in the center of his chest, causing him to stumble backward. At that exact moment, another man came rushing out of the room.

He went to the side of the hall and threw a stiff sort of clothesline that knocked Ellington down in a heap. Mackenzie took a shooter's stance just as both men noticed her at the end of the hallway.

"Stop right there," she bellowed.

Both men froze for a moment. Behind them, Ellington slowly started to get to his feet. As he made it to his knees, the man with the bat threw it hard at Mackenzie. While she sidestepped it and the bat tore a chunk out of the wall two feet in front of her, both men dashed to the left, through an open door along the hallway. The first one made it inside but Ellington was able to grab the leg of the second man. He wrapped his arm around the man's leg and twisted, throwing him into the doorframe.

Mackenzie started forward and reached the room just as Ellington threw himself on the man. He was pinning the suspect's arms behind him, easily overpowering the much smaller man. Mackenzie looked into the room and saw that the third man had opened a window on the far side of the room. He was currently pushing out the screen and throwing a leg over to the outside.

Mackenzie dashed into the room and reached for the man, not seeing the need to fire a shot yet (even though he *had* thrown a baseball bat at her less than ten seconds ago). She barely missed him, her hand grazing the back of his shirt as he made it out. Mackenzie nearly went after him but then saw Officer Roberts and the other policeman getting out of the third patrol car. Roberts was already racing after the man and there was no way he was going to escape.

When Mackenzie turned back toward the hallway, she saw that Ellington had his suspect pinned against the wall. Ellington looked to be in a bit of pain, making Mackenzie wonder just how hard he'd been struck by the baseball bat.

"You good here?" she asked.

"Oh yeah, we're great," Ellington said, leading the man into the living room with both arms twisted behind his back.

Mackenzie ran through the living room, passing by the front door where Bateman currently had Fowley in cuffs and pressed against the wall. She made her way out onto the porch and saw that Roberts and the other officer had tackled the third man to the ground. He was putting up a fight, but Deputy Wickline was currently racing through the snow to assist.

Mackenzie turned back to the living room just as Bateman shoved Fowley down onto his couch. He grunted in pain, landing awkwardly on his right arm, pulled behind his back and cuffed to the left.

Bateman sat down beside him and gave him an angry look. Mackenzie had seen him irritated and defeated but not angry. It was actually rather menacing.

"You yelled 'backup plan,'" Bateman said. "You want to tell me what the *first* plan was?"

Fowley said nothing. He bit his lip defiantly and shook his head.

Mackenzie stood in front of him and looked down at him. She wanted to get angry as well but knew it would be much more impactful if she was calm and collected. "You attacked me, an FBI agent. Then this genius here," she said, hitching a thumb to the man Ellington was holding, "hit another agent in the chest with a baseball bat and then threw it at me. So you're already in a shitload of trouble. If you make this harder by staying quiet, it's just going to be worse for you."

Fowley seemed to think about this. Mackenzie saw fear starting to take root in his eyes as he looked around the room.

"Be smart," Mackenzie said. "Help yourself. Tell us where the women are."

"There are no women," he said, but his voice was thin and wavering.

"Bullshit," Bateman said. "How about Missy Hale? Crystal Hall? Oh, and Delores Manning, who outsmarted your dumb ass. Ring any bells?"

He looked confused but still indignant. He said nothing, keeping his eyes dead ahead.

"I don't know what you're talking about," Fowley said. There was relief in his voice now but he was still clearly nervous.

Bateman looked at Mackenzie.

"What do you think?" Bateman asked.

She didn't want to play her whole hand in front of Fowley so she simply gave a lazy shrug. "Take him in. Innocent men sure as hell don't randomly attack FBI agents."

"You heard the lady," Bateman said. "On your feet, Fowley. You're under arrest."

***

Deputy Wickline and the officer that Mackenzie did not know rode back to the station with the three suspects in tow. Mackenzie watched things play out as Fowley and his partners were placed into the back of the patrol cars and Wickline and the other officer carefully navigated both cars out of the driveway.

143

Mackenzie had elected to stay behind to search the property for evidence, certain that Fowley was not their man. Ellington remained with her and, for reasons Mackenzie had yet to determine, Bateman and Roberts also stayed behind.

As Mackenzie looked around the backyard, using flashlights taken from the patrol cars, Bateman sidled up next to her. "You think this is our guy?"

"I'm not sure," she said.

Bateman made a small *hmmm* sound in the back of his throat as they continued searching. As they came to the rear of the yard, their flashlights and the scant moonlight revealed a small gardener's shed. Ellington approached it cautiously, still visibly shaken from the attack with the bat. He opened up the door, revealing the inside.

There were two cattle containers inside the shed. One was smaller, perhaps big enough to carry two pigs. The other was quite large.

Bateman hurried inside and looked into the crates. Unable to open them because they were locked, he shined his flashlight through the slats along the front of both of them. "Empty," he said.

Further investigating turned up a crate filled with pornography magazines, several old dog collars, two dead lawn mowers, and an old deteriorated dog kennel that had been taken apart and tossed in a heap into the back corner.

"Sheriff," Mackenzie said, "Delores Manning says she saw two, maybe three large sheds. This doesn't match that description at all."

"You're right," he said. "But then again, that was testimony coming from a woman with trauma to the head—*while* under hypnosis. Forgive me for not accepting every word of it."

"He's right," Roberts said. She spoke so infrequently that it genuinely took Mackenzie by surprise. "He's guilty. Why else would he attack? Why else would he have two other people here that knew right away what he meant by *backup plan*?"

Mackenzie wanted to argue it, knowing that everything she was saying held up under scrutiny. So many times in the past, her gut instinct had been right. When others had thought the case was closed, some other part of her had insisted the hunt was not over.

*Maybe this is the guy,* she thought, daring to feel victorious. *Maybe we got the bastard.*

"Okay," she said. "Let's say Fowley *is* our guy. Where are the women?"

"I'd like to find that out for myself," Bateman said. "And I'm sure as hell not going to find out by standing out here in the cold.

We're sharing a car now. I say we get back to the station and grill this asshole."

Mackenzie looked to the shed and the looming white forest behind it. She then looked to Ellington and saw that he appeared to be torn. He gave her a shrug, a defeated gesture that did not suit him. "Sounds good to me," he said.

She'd expected him to have her back. In a way, she supposed, he *did.* While it was clear he felt that something here was not quite lining up, he also knew that it would only cause more turmoil to get into a heated argument. Plus, the way he was grimacing with each breath indicated that maybe the attack he'd suffered from the baseball bat had been harsher than it had seemed.

Bateman wasted no time in walking back to the single car remaining in Ed Fowley's driveway. Mackenzie followed behind, taking one final glance back at the yard. The night falling on the snow looked ominous, yet, in an odd way, welcoming. It made it seem as if there were still plenty of secrets left out there to be uncovered.

But for the moment, she still allowed herself to hope. *We got him,* she thought, trying out the words. *Maybe it's all over.*

# CHAPTER TWENTY EIGHT

Mackenzie was pacing anxiously in the observation room, watching three scenes unfold on small black-and-white monitors in front of her. Fowley and his two accomplices had been given their own individual interrogation rooms. She'd elected to sit out of the interrogations for now. She was too frustrated and knew she would not be an effective interrogator if her mind was preoccupied. Instead, she watched as Bateman, Deputy Wickline, and Ellington questioned the three men.

Fowley had made it clear that he was not going to talk. Unfortunately for him, the same could not be said for his two accomplices. She watched as Ellington went to work on the younger-looking accomplice, a twenty-three-year-old named Jackson Randall.

"We ran your ID," Ellington said. "We know you have a clean record. So if you can play ball, I'll personally see to it that you get the absolute minimum sentence for striking an FBI agent with a bat—perhaps even just a monetary fine. But if you're difficult, you can go ahead and serve those twenty years or so with Fowley."

Mackenzie killed the feeds on the other two monitors and listened solely to Randall. "I don't know what the hell this is all about!" Randall said.

"So you mean to tell me that you have no idea who Delores Manning, Crystal Hall, Naomi Nyles, or Missy Hale are?"

"No way, man. Ed...he wasn't into it all that much. He just kind of lined up the real bad guys with cages. You know?"

"No, I don't know."

"Some dude out of Nicaragua. I don't know. He's living in Vegas now or something, I think. He used Ed's crates to get the girls from one place to the other. The cattle crates work so much better because...ah shit, man...because it was easier to tie the girls down."

"What girls?" Ellington said. "I thought you said there *were* no girls."

"Like I just said, Ed never dealt with the girls. Just the crates."

"And we're talking about kidnapped girls?"

"I don't know. I guess. He used the word *trafficking* a few times."

"How many women were there?" Ellington asked.

"I don't know. Honestly. I only know of two for sure."

"Who were they sold to?"

"I don't know. Again, that was all Ed. That part of it…it sort of pissed me off."

"How long has he been at this?" Ellington asked, his voice getting louder.

"A little less than a year, I think."

"And you are absolutely positive he hasn't been taking women from off the roads around here?"

"If he has been, I didn't know about it."

"So why did he need two partners if he was just selling crates to these men?"

"I was just the tech guy. Making sure e-mails and money couldn't be traced. Henry, the other guy, just came on. I don't know why. I think he was a friend of the guy in Vegas."

"So we're talking about human trafficking?" Ellington asked, now in Randall's face.

It was at that point that Randall started to cry. He simply broke down in front of Ellington, perhaps broken down from the weight of what he had been assisting with.

And while everything she heard was terrible, Mackenzie became more and more aware that Ed Fowley was not their man.

*So much for feeling victorious,* she thought.*Have I missed this all along? Our guy is too cautious, if not a bit formulaic. But what if he's been taking these women to…sell? What if there's some other motive behind it than simple control? The two crimes between these two creeps may not be linked, but it's something to consider.*

Someone knocked on the already-open observation room door behind her. She turned and saw Roberts entering with a cup of coffee. She handed it to Mackenzie and said, "Can you believe it? This fucking town…as if drugs weren't bad enough."

"Is this a whole new issue for Bent Creek?" Mackenzie asked.

"Human trafficking? Yes."

"Officer Roberts, do you think you could arrange to have me borrow a patrol car in the next few minutes? Preferably with chains on the tires?"

"Sure. Where are you going?"

"Back out there. If we now have evidence of human trafficking in the area, even if it's just the selling of transport crates, there's a whole new level of evidence to search for. Maybe I'll take a better look at the crates or start looking into Fowley's list of lost loves to see what they have to offer."

"But it seems like this is our guy," Roberts said. "And it's cold, dark, and snowing. Can we just let it rest?"

"Sure. And if we ever find these women and they ask why they were left in the cold to get frostbitten, I'll tell them it was your idea."

"Fine," Roberts spat. "I'll make the request."

Mackenzie exited the observation room with Roberts and headed down a few doors to Interrogation Room 2, where Ellington was still at work. She knocked on the door and Ellington came to the small window to peer out at her.

He opened the door and stepped out for a moment. Randall's cries seeped out in that instant, the sounds of a man filled with regrets.

"Can you believe this?" Ellington asked.

"It's pretty terrible. I feel like we came into town and swept up all this dirty stuff that had been lying hidden for so long."

"I almost feel bad about it," Ellington said. "Anyway, what's up?"

"I think I'm going to head back out and poke around the back roads. Those women...they're still out there somewhere while we're grilling three men that have no idea where they are."

"Let me finish up here and I'll come with you," he offered.

"No. Take your time here. Another half an hour or so and you guys can maybe bust up an entire trafficking ring. Stay on this angle. I'll only be a few hours at most."

"Well, please be careful," he said. For a moment, she saw the longing she had seen in his eyes the previous night in his motel room.

"I will," she said. "Awesome work in there, by the way."

"Oh, I *do* have my moments."

She rewarded him with a small laugh as she turned back for the front of the building. As promised, Roberts had a car ready and waiting for her. When she got behind the wheel, the car was already warm. Wasting no time, she headed back out into Bent Creek just as night settled down over the blanket of white that had covered the town.

At least three women were out there, possibly cold and certainly afraid.

*But what if they* aren't *here?* she thought. *What if the abductor has relocated them? Or what if he* killed *them after Delores Manning escaped?*

She couldn't think like that, though. In fact, she *refused* to think like that.

She carefully made her way down the main stretch, away from the police department. She headed for the ever-winding back roads that snaked back into the forest as if the road itself was trying to strangle the life out of the snow.

## CHAPTER TWENTY NINE

Mackenzie headed back to Ed Fowley's house, driving down Skinner's Reach Road simply to have a starting point to her search. There was also something gnawing at her—something she had seen or sensed while at Fowley's that she hadn't had time to process. She stopped the car in front of his driveway, trying to get the lay of the land and a sense of how the snow would impede her search.

Mackenzie started down his driveway and parked where she had before. She walked directly out to the barn, giving it another look. The crates offered no evidence at all. Without a deep investigation with a forensics team, she wouldn't be able to tell if the crates had been used for dogs, barn animals, or kidnapped women.

She walked back out into the snow. She looked at all of the prints they stomped into the ground earlier and then looked out to the woods.

That's when she saw the faint glow through the trees. She'd spotted it earlier but had been so focused on getting into the barn that she had not taken the time to consider it. *A neighbor,* she thought.

It was a long shot, but she thought a neighbor might know enough about Fowley to eliminate him from the list of suspects. While she understood why the local PD might be convinced that Fowley was their man, Mackenzie knew for certain that the profiles simply didn't match up.

She got back into her car and made her way out of Fowley's driveway, managing to only go skidding in the snow on two occasions. As she reached the main road, her doubts resurfaced. She supposed it was possible that there was some sort of connection between what Ed Fowley was doing and what her guy was up to. It would be rather coincidental in any other case so why was she fighting it now?

Roughly a quarter of a mile down Skinner's Reach Road, a driveway appeared on her left—the same side of the road Fowley's house was on. This would be Fowley's neighbor in the rural sense of the word. She could see that little glow she had seen through the trees in Fowley's yard, only clearer now. Mackenzie couldn't help but wonder if the neighbor might have some insight into Fowley or his connections. What had the neighbor seen as Fowley had sold these containers? What might they know about shady dealings and events on these back roads?

She turned onto the driveway and found that it was rather short. A small house came into view right away, faint light spilling through almost every window inside. The snow made it look quaint and inviting.

It was 8:10 when she parked her car and killed the engine in the small snowed-over driveway. A beaten up pickup truck was the only other vehicle. She looked beyond the house and saw two sheds. This raised no real alarms, as nearly every property she had stepped foot on since coming to Bent Creek had held some form of barn or shed. She walked up to the ramshackle porch and the Thomas Kinkaid comparison ended. The place was in a mild state of disrepair, the porch nothing more than thrown together boards and warped railings.

As she made her way onto the porch, she heard something weird in the distance. At first, she thought it was just the wind or maybe even something squealing beneath the porch. She then realized that it was the sound of dogs whining—puppies to be exact. Apparently a dog on this property had just delivered a litter.

The porch groaned under her weight as she knocked on the door. Due to the shoddy nature of the house, she had been expecting an older man to answer the door, perhaps a hermit that spent most of his afternoons with a twelve-pack of beer and a baseball game on the radio. So when a forty-something man with a handsome smile answered, she was a little surprised. He had a lumberjack sort of build, with massive shoulders and huge upper arms.

"Hey there," the man said, clearly confused.

"Hi. I'm so sorry to bother you at such an hour," Mackenzie said. "I'm Agent White with the FBI. I was wondering if you had a moment to answer some questions about your neighbor."

"My neighbor? The closest person I know of is Ed Fowley."

"That's exactly who I mean," Mackenzie said.

"Sure then, yes, come on in," the man said. He seemed very hesitant to move back from his door but when he finally did, he was as cordial as could be expected from someone receiving a visit from the FBI after 8:00 p.m.

As Mackenzie entered the living room, she saw that the inside of the place was not at all like the outside. Everything was clean and tidied up. She sat down on the side of the couch against the right wall while the man sat in his recliner.

"You know, I already spoke with the FBI earlier today," the man said.

"You did?"

"Sure did. Fella named Arrington, I think. Or maybe it was Ellington."

"Ellington," Mackenzie said. "That's my partner."

"So I take it things are still at a stand-still?"

"I can't discuss the details of the case, but I *would* appreciate your cooperation in answering questions about Mr. Fowley. What is *your* name?"

"Harry Givens," he said.

"And how long have you lived in this proximity to Mr. Fowler?"

"Twelve years. He moved in over there after some legal trouble if I remember correctly. Quiet guy, really. I've only ever sat down and had a chat with him a few times."

"Did you know about his legal troubles in the past?"

"No, I sort of just keep to myself, you know? Not one for gossip."

"And what do you do for a living?" she asked.

"This and that," he said. "In the spring and summer I make fair money with my meager crops. When things get busy at the slaughterhouse during peak season, they bring me on."

He was pleasant enough. He smiled when he spoke and had expressive eyes. There was dull look about him, though. As cruel as it sounded, she got the feeling that he might not be all there upstairs. Still, he was charming and seemed comfortable around her even though she was an FBI agent visiting at such a late hour.

"Let me ask you…do you know a young lady named Crystal Hall?"

He nodded and gave a mischievous grin. "I do, I do. And not for the best of reasons. She has a reputation, you know."

"Word has it she was sleeping with Ed Fowley at one time. Did you know that?"

"I did," he said. "And it was…well, *regrettable* the way people took that. Two people like being around each other. So what? Maybe they loved each other."

"Yes, but Mr. Fowley was married at the time."

"Marriage," Harry said with a chuckle. "Who has time for that? It kills love, you know? And that's all we really want. To be loved."

The conversation was taking a strange turn. Little alarms started to sound in Mackenzie's head.

"Mr. Givens, I noticed you have two sheds out back. Would you mind if I had a look in them?"

Harry sighed, as if he were irritated. "I went through all of this earlier today," he said. "Your partner already looked in them."

"He did?"

"Yes. I was splitting wood when he came. I had to come back inside and fetch the keys."

"Forgive me, but I'd appreciate it if I could just have a look."

"Think you're a better agent than he is?" he asked with a grin.

"No, we just think differently."

"Honestly, I'd rather you didn't. I'm a private man. I try to keep to myself. And now someone else in town fucks up and I get hassled for it. Tell me...this partner of yours. Do you like him?"

She stuttered a bit, not expecting that question. "I don't see what—"

"Do you *love* him?"

"Mr. Givens, I—

She was interrupted by the buzzing of her cell phone from within her pocket. "Excuse me, please," she said, pulling the phone from her pocket.

She had received a text message from a number she did not know. She read it and did her very best to act as if she was unaffected by it. The truth of the matter was, though, it took an incredible amount of willpower not to jump off of the couch.

The text message was from Delores Manning. It read:

**That weird noise I'd heard—puppies. It was puppies.**

Mackenzie pocketed the cell phone as casually as she could. When she had come up onto Harry Givens's porch, she'd heard something odd...something that had taken her a while to place. And in the end, she had thought it had been the sound of a litter of puppies. Young puppies, likely still scrambling over one another to get to their mother's milk.

"Do you happen to know what Mr. Fowley did for employment?" Mackenzie asked, hoping to seem collected and trying to drag the conversation back to something resembling normalcy.

She couldn't see any sign that he suspected anything. She thought about texting Ellington to get him out here but was afraid that might seem too obvious. She could, of course, simply jump to her feet, pull her gun, and arrest him right then and there. But if Harry Givens *was* the guilty party and she took such action, he may not be very cooperative in telling them where the women were.

*Got to make sure we know where the women are before I try to take him on alone. I need to get in touch with Ellington.*

153

She looked around the house, comparing it to the outside. So clean, so tidy. It looked almost out of place. A hairbrush sat on the arm of his recliner. An old denim shirt was hanging on the edge of it.

*Denim shirt. Oh my god...Delores reported the same thing under hypnosis.*

In a flash so quick it made her heart seem to float for a moment, Mackenzie got to her feet and drew her gun. Harry rocked back in the recliner, his eyes growing wide. An almost comical look of surprise washed over his face as he timidly raised his hands into the air.

"Whoa, whoa, what the hell is this?"

"Get out of the chair and put your hands on your head. Do it slowly."

He smiled at her then, that same smile that made her think he was perhaps a little mentally unbalanced. Still, he did as she asked. He slowly laced his hands over his head, those massive arms hidden by a baggy sweater but no less intimidating.

"Think you've got it figured out?" he said. "Good for you. But you will never understand it. Never. The need to be loved. The need to be—"

"On your knees," she said.

He obeyed her here as well. Slowly, with her gun still trained on him, Mackenzie reached into her inner coat pocket with her left hand. She pulled out her phone and quickly pulled up Ellington's number. She called it but only got a series of clicks.

She briefly eyed the display while doing her best to stay focused on Harry Givens. *No service.* There was only one little dot of signal and here in these woods, that seemed as good as totally empty. It was a wonder the text made it through.

"Calling your partner?" Harry asked. "Are you frightened of me? Scared to try to take me in on your own?"

"Shut up," she said.

Her eyes remained on Harry the entire time, the gun no more than six inches from his head. He started to shift his hand, and she barked:

"On your knees! Turn around and raise your hands slowly where I can see them. In the air. NOW!"

Her heart pounded as she watched the man she felt certain was the kidnapper. He slowly turned and did as she said.

She reached back and pulled out her cuffs. She leaned over and slapped one end on one wrist, wrenching one arm behind his back.

She then lowered her gun just a bit as she reached up to wrench the other wrist down.

And that was her mistake.

Suddenly, Harry Givens was moving. His right hand came slightly down and over in an arc. Mackenzie suddenly saw something shiny in his hand and that was enough cause for her to pull the trigger.

She knew right away that her shot went high. He had moved too damned fast and her flinching had caused her aim to waver. Rather than hitting Harry high in the shoulder, she barely grazed him. She could actually see the fabric of the sweatshirt tear.

With his free hand, he swung down, and she saw now that he had been hiding a small hammer up his sleeve. It slid down, its shaft fitting perfectly into the palm of his hand, and then he caught it and swung for her knee.

Her knee exploded in pain. She screamed, buckled, and went to the floor. Her phone clattered beside her. She raised her gun, but before she could get her arm all the way up, Harry threw a knee onto her chest. The air went out of her with painful force as his hands found her wrists and tore the gun away from her.

He was then kneeling over her, a leg to either side of her chest. She saw the hammer in his hand, and he was bringing it down again.

This time, she was able to block the blow. His force was incredible, though. While she managed to block off the hammer, she still caught a forearm to the face.

Then the hammer was coming down again. This time it caught her in the left side. She powered through the pain and threw an elbow up before he could raise his arm again. It caught him in the soft padding of his underarm but knocked him back just enough so that she could scramble out from beneath him.

She tried getting to her feet but her left leg wouldn't support her. She went to the floor and right away felt the hammer striking her again. This time it caught her in the back. She let out a shout as a flare of agony swept through her entire back. She felt something give, a twinge of sorts that felt like a pinch.

A pins-and-needles sensation flared through her entire body. She let out a scream of pain that surprised her. For a terrifying moment, she worried that he had done some irreparable damage to her spine…that she'd try to fight back only to realize that she was paralyzed.

Fortunately, she could still move. But slowly. So slowly that she was unable to avoid the next attack. This one was going for her head. She managed to move her neck just in time; rather than smashing into her forehead, the hammer bounced off of her temple. Pain exploded across her face and she started to see white flecks.

She had no idea where her gun was.

Mackenzie felt a cold, creeping dread wash over her. She had an awful rush of inevitability. She was helpless now, too wounded to fight back against this monster. If he didn't kill her outright, things were about to get bad very quickly for her.

With her world spinning, she reached out for the only thing she saw: her phone. She grabbed it with a shaking hand and began to type:

**Fowley's nei**

She felt another blow of the hammer, and she involuntarily pressed the SEND button, delivering—she hoped—the portion of a text to Ellington.

Harry stomped down on the phone. It shattered, a few pieces flicking Mackenzie in the face.

She tried scrambling to her feet or at least away from him. Maybe she could get to her gun while he was distracted with beating the hell out of her. But it felt impossible to draw a breath. Her ribs ached, her back felt like it was going numb, and the right side of her face was a mess of pain. And just as she was able to register all of this, there was a new pain…one that seemed to come out of nowhere.

Givens was grabbing her by the hair, jerking her to her feet. The pain was too unbearable to fight against it. She had to get to her feet to lessen the pain. Just as her scrambling feet found the floor, she felt herself shoved hard into the wall. The right side of her face caught the impact and this time, she couldn't help it. She let out a cry of pain that she was ashamed of but *shit*…this was getting bad.

She was dazed, dizzy, and knew that she could pass out at any moment. She felt him pulling her by the hair again and she did her best to fight against him. He swatted her hand away and pushed her again. It all happened so quickly that the world was a blur, her dizziness only making it worse. So when the push sent her sprawling forward without a wall to stop her, she was confused when she continued to fall.

She fell hard on something wooden, something cold. *Outside,* she thought. *He opened the door and pushed me outside.*

She reached out for the railing. He was there right away, grabbing her arm and twisting it. She was being pushed forward, unable to fall because his grip on her right arm was so tight. He was leading her through the snow, around the side of his house. The cold bit into her, not nearly as sharp as the world of pain that engulfed her body.

*The cold might be the best thing for me. Might keep me from passing out.*

As her dizziness continued to tilt the world, she saw the two sheds coming into view. In the world of tilted white, the sheds looked almost abstract.

*What the hell are you doing?* she asked herself. *Fight back. Get your shit together and fight back!*

She tried wrangling her right arm free but the mere motion of it sent a flare of terrible pain along her back. *Something's out of whack back there. Something bad...fighting back might not even be an option.*

She tried halting her feet, digging them into the snow to stop Givens from moving her forward, but that didn't work either. When her knees locked up, her back bent forward and sent another flare of pain racing up her spine. She tried to endure it, locking her legs and holding it as long as she could.

Givens responded by yanking her arm up behind her and driving one of his elbows into the center of her back. The pain was immense. Mackenzie would have fallen to her knees if he hadn't been holding her arm.

Before she knew it, he was shoving her hard against the closest shed. He fumbled with a lock, opened the door, and she fell in.

She tried getting to her feet, but he was on her again. He had gone back to her hair, sending ripples of pain along her scalp and flaring up the pain along the right side of her face. The shed was dark so as he led her into it, she could see very little. He was leading her to something square-shaped that seemed to stick out in the darkness. Whatever it was, it had some sort of a door on it that he fumbled with, using his free hand while still pulling her hair with the other.

*A cattle crate,* she thought.

He put his mouth to her left ear and whispered in what was supposed to be a comforting way. "The fight in you...I like it. I think you're my favorite so far. I can't wait to break you in."

With that, he shoved her hard inside the crate. Blindly, and with the last reserve of courage and strength she had, Mackenzie stuck her left arm out and caught the side of the door. When he tried pushing her in, she grabbed his hand. He pulled away, but not

157

before she latched on to his thumb, gripped it, and twisted as hard as she could.

There was a sharp *click* as his thumb broke. He screamed in pain and in one last act of violence, kicked her hard in the back. She screamed, the pain nearly unbearable, and went sailing into the crate. She collapsed against the back, her entire body nothing but a knot of pain that radiated from her spine.

He slammed the front of the crate. She was enveloped in darkness, with the exception of three rectangular shapes in front of her where the softer darkness of the shed came through.

He was still whimpering on the outside and gave her crate a hard kick. "You broke my thumb," he said. "I'll see that you pay for that. With the others, it'll be nice and romantic. But with you...I'm going to make you bleed."

With that, he stormed away. She could hear him go, his footfalls like thunder in the shed. He slammed the shed door closed behind him and then there was only the sound of his footfalls retreating in the snow.

Mackenzie was shuddering, trying to make sense of the pain in her back. Worse, she felt naked. She had no phone and her gun was gone. She was trapped, unarmed, and very likely hurt worse than she had ever been in her life.

# CHAPTER THIRTY

When some semblance of rational thought centered itself in her mind again, Mackenzie took a moment to go over her condition. She went over her injuries one by one, trying to take on the role of a physician.

First, her left knee. She knew it was not broken or fractured. But he had definitely done some sort of damage there. She couldn't even put half of her weight on that leg without the knee buckling. Then there was her face. She could already feel swelling there. There were signs of blood and as far as she could tell, she could still work her jaw just fine, though it was a bit sore. So nothing serious there. Next, her ribs. The soreness from his kick was already fading so there was nothing to be concerned about there. But it was her back that had her the most concerned. It hurt to sit up straight, so she could only imagine what it might be like to stand. She could move her arms and legs—other than the hurt knee—just fine, so she assumed whatever injuries she'd suffered were not too serious.

*Maybe it's just muscular,* she thought. *Or maybe I strained or pulled something. Either way, getting out of here is going to be a bitch. I can only hope my text to Ellington went through before that asshole trashed my phone.*

She scooted to the front of the container and looked out. She could just barely see the edges of the shed door. She then backed away and tried to make out the back of the door to the container. She could see nothing, so she ran her fingers along the edges of it. Within a few seconds, she was pretty sure the entire locking mechanism was inside the door and along the outside.

As she did her best to think of a way out, a voice interrupted her. It was frail and almost a whisper but still scared the hell out of her.

"H—hello?"

Mackenzie went back to the front of the container. She looked back out through the slats but saw no one. She was pretty sure the voice had come from the left, just out of sight.

"Hello," Mackenzie said. "Who's there?"

"My name is Missy. Is he—"

She stopped here, as if uncertain of whether or not she wanted to finish asking the question.

"Missy *Hale*?" Mackenzie asked.

"Yes. How did you know?"

"My name is Mackenzie White. I'm an FBI agent. We've been looking for you."

Missy let out a choked little laugh that lacked humor. "Well, I guess you found me."

"What has he done to you?" Mackenzie asked, dreading the answer and what it might mean.

"Nothing yet," she said. "He put a gag around my mouth earlier today. Another agent was here. When the agent left and he came back to take the gag off, he talked to me like he…like he was trying to be sweet. Talked about making love to me."

"But he hasn't physically hurt you?"

"Not since braining me with a hammer on the side of the road."

Mackenzie noticed that the more Missy Hale spoke, the more coherent she seemed. She also seemed to be getting rather angry. Silence fell between them and Mackenzie listened for the sound of puppies—the sound Delores Manning had heard. But they had fallen quiet for now, nursing or asleep elsewhere on the property.

"Do you know if there are others here?" Mackenzie asked.

"I think there might be at least one more," she said. "I'm not sure, though. I always heard him talking somewhere else…somewhere outside of this shed."

"Have you heard dogs?" Mackenzie asked. "Puppies, maybe?"

"I thought I heard some little squeaking sort of noises like a small animals. I guess it could have been puppies." She stopped here, and then, her voice returning to its low and vulnerable state, she added, "Are we going to get out of here?"

"I'm certainly going to try. My partner may be on the way at any moment."

*If that damned text went through…*

She started to wonder what might happen if the text didn't make it through. She figured they'd give her about an hour to an hour and a half before they started to wonder why she hadn't yet returned or, at the very least, called. Another half an hour or so would pass before anyone went out looking for her—and with the way things were going at the station with Ed Fowley locked up, it would likely be Ellington. And then, of course, there was the matter of finding her. And if he had already been out here to Givens's property today, this would probably be the last place he'd check…if at all

In other words, if that text didn't go through, she was screwed. And even if it *did* make it through, there were no guarantees. She hadn't even been able to send the entire message.

As much as she hated the thought, it was all on Ellington now. All she could do was wait. And that was somehow the most painful thing of all.

# CHAPTER THIRTY ONE

Ellington was sitting in the conference room with Roberts and Wickline when his phone buzzed in his pocket. Bateman was still trying to milk information out of Fowley, whereas Ellington had just about everything he needed. He, like Mackenzie, was starting to have some doubts that Fowley was the man they were looking for. He was in the middle of looking through Fowley's old police reports when his phone broke his concentration.

It was a text from Mackenzie. But not a text that made much sense. Right away, the peculiar nature of it sent him into panic mode. He got to his feet, rereading the strange message.

**Fowley's nei**

*What the hell is that supposed mean?*
Whatever it meant, it seemed to be an incomplete text. Something was either wrong or she was in an extreme hurry. Neither option was a good one.

Leaving the conference room, he called her. The line clicked uselessly in his ear. It did not even go to voicemail.

He ran to the front of the office, to the reception area. He saw Roberts and a few other officers sorting through paperwork. "Roberts, I need a car."

"You, too? You know Agent White already took one."

"Yes, I do. I need to meet her. It might be urgent. So can you please just loan me a car?"

She seemed to sense the urgency in his voice because her somewhat annoyed look evaporated at once. "Yes, of course. Is everything okay?"

"I don't know," he said.

But he looked back down to the text and felt worry churning in his stomach.

***

He had no idea what the text was supposed to say but the fact that Fowley's name was in it directed Ellington back to Skinner's Reach Road. He carefully drove the borrowed patrol car down Fowley's driveway for the second time that night. He peered across the snowy yard and the snow-capped trees. His headlights were still on and the car's heater was working overtime.

162

He parked the car and wasted no time going into Fowley's house. He looked everywhere, rummaging through the house in a hurry. He called out to her several times but got no answer. It took less than three minutes for him to realize that she was not in the house. He headed back outside and continued his search in the shed outside.

Again, there was no sign of her.

He went back outside and scanned the yard. There were so many prints from their earlier trip out here that it was hard to tell if any of them were new. While the snow had almost stopped coming down completely, it had already done its damage.

As he scanned the yard, he noticed the faint glow of light through the stripped trees. He supposed that was Fowley's neighbor, Harry Givens—the fellow he had visited today.

*Two sheds in his backyard,* he thought.

The contents of Mackenzie's text came back to him like a slap to the brain.

**Fowley's nei**

*Was she trying to type the word* neighbor?

"Shit," he said.

He sprinted back to the patrol car and shifted into reverse. He left Ed Fowley's driveway in such a hurry that the back end fishtailed in the snow. When he finally had it corrected, he sped up the driveway, kicking up snow and slipping tires the entire way.

*This is it,* he thought. *Givens is the guy.*

He'd ignored his instincts earlier in the day. He'd be damned if he'd do it again. He didn't even bother with trying to be discreet, even though he knew that was the smartest play. He sped through the snow, covering the brief space between the two driveways as quickly as possible. He turned onto Givens's property and again started down a driveway he'd already been down once today.

He parked the car, leaving the engine running. He walked quickly to the porch, drawing his Glock. He heard soft music playing inside, some old honkytonk nonsense.

On the porch, Ellington kept his eyes trained on the single window that shone out onto the porch. He stayed low, waiting for a figure to appear in front of the window. It took less than two minutes. Harry Givens walked by the window, holding a glass.

Knowing that Givens was in the living room, Ellington summoned up all the anger he felt in that moment. He used it to draw back his leg and deliver a savage kick to the door. His aim

163

was dead on, landing along the solid bulk of the locking mechanism within the door. The door flew backward, tearing from the bottom hinge and nearly falling to the floor inside.

He trained his gun to the right and saw Givens standing there. A look of shock was on his face. He dropped the glass of water he'd been drinking to the floor.

"Nice to see you again," Ellington said. "This time, I think I'm going to have you unlock that shed out there."

"Are you kidding me?" Givens said. "You can't just bust in here without a warrant. I know the law!"

"I doubt that," Ellington said. "If you knew the law, you wouldn't have three women locked up in that shed out back. One of which is my partner. So I'm going to tell you this one time. Take me out there and unlock it. If you don't, I'll blow out your knee and claim I shot you while trying to escape."

He watched as Givens was clearly trying to think of a way out of this. The confidence Ellington had seen in his eyes earlier was gone. Now he understood the weight of his crimes and he was beginning to crumble.

"Okay," he said, near tears. "Okay."

Ellington kept his aim on Givens as he led him to the busted down front door and back out into the snow. They marched through the yard toward the shed. Ellington took a great deal of pleasure in the sight of Givens limping a bit. He wondered if it was from the injury Delores Manning had doled out. He took similar pleasure in watching his hands trembling as he found the key on a crowded key ring and unlocked the shed door. Givens inserted the key and turned it, popping the lock open. He hesitated, as if unsure of what to do next.

"Open the door," Ellington barked.

Givens jumped at the tone in his voice and did as he asked. Ellington saw that the bastard was actually crying as he led him into the shed.

"Are there lights in here?" Ellington asked.

"Yeah. On the post to your right."

Still keeping the gun targeted at Givens, Ellington felt around on the post and finally found a light switch. Two overhead bulbs came to life overhead, revealing the rest of the shed. From her cattle container, Missy Hale let out a breathy "Oh, thank God!"

Ellington took a quick inventory of the shed. There were two of the containers. One was pressed all the way against the back wall. The other was nearly positioned in the center of the shed. The idea that he had been standing less than fifteen feet away from it about eleven hours ago made him feel sick to his stomach.

He also saw black spray paint on a little workbench along the far wall. Beside it was a box of old glass vases and bowls. *That's how he got Delores Manning,* Ellington thought. *How many more did he plan to get like that?*

"Open the cages," Ellington said.

"Please," Givens pleaded. "You have to understand. I—"

"Shut your mouth and open those cages."

Givens approached Missy's cage, his hands still trembling. He reached out for the bar that had been slid across the gate. It held a smaller vertical bar in place, serving as the locking system. Yet when he pulled on the bar, nothing happened.

"Don't fuck with me," Ellington said. "Open it!"

"I'm trying," Givens whined. It's stuck or something. This one always had a stick to it."

Ellington stepped forward and pushed Givens into the front of the cage. "Stop playing around and do it. I already want to shoot you. I *dare* you to give me another reason."

Givens was finally able to undo the latch, spring the sheet of chicken wire inside, and then push the gate open. Inside, Missy Hale whimpered her relief.

And then she did something totally unexpected. She dove at Givens, letting out a scream of primal fury. They both went to the ground and when they did, Givens took complete advantage.

"You bitch," he hissed as he rolled on top of her. His hands went to her neck and he bore down with all of his weight.

Ellington placed his hands on Givens's shoulders and pulled him off. He threw him to the floor hard and went into a motion to drop a knee into Givens's crotch. As he dropped down, though, Givens brought a knee up, catching Ellington in the stomach. He wheeled back a bit, tripping over Missy's legs.

He stumbled back, feeling foolish and taken off of his feet. By the time he regained his footing, Givens was coming at him. He pushed Ellington hard against the wall, knocking the box of glass bowls from the bench. Givens found a two-by-four propped against the wall and was now rearing back as if it were a baseball bat.

With no other choice, Ellington fired the Glock. It took Givens in the right arm but it did not slow him down. He fired a second shot, this one taking him in the center of the chest.

This second shot slowed him momentarily but he continued to come rushing at Ellington, driving a shoulder into his stomach. Ellington brought the butt of the Glock down on the base of

Givens's neck three times in quick succession, making him rear back.

As Ellington advanced, taking a shooter's stance, Givens acted quickly. He drew the two-by-four up in a hard arc, catching Ellington in the chest. It felt like he had been hit by a car as he staggered back. Givens came again, raising the board. Ignoring the pain, Ellington threw out a hard jab directly into Givens's left knee. He then delivered two punches to his stomach but still, Givens would not go down. He swung the two-by-four again. In return, Ellington fired a third shot.

The shot blew the board apart, but not before the board slammed into Ellington's wrists. The Glock went flying immediately after being fired and Givens screamed. Either the bullet or the splintered wood had sliced open the side of his brow. Blood was pouring out of it but still, the bastard was coming for him.

Givens raised the small portion of board that remained. Ellington could only draw his arm up, hoping to deliver a punch before Givens. But before he could do so, the board slammed into his arm. Electric pain shot up his arm as Givens drew the board back again. Ellington protected his head in a boxer's defensive stance. Although it did save his head, there was a splintering noise as two fingers on his left hand were broken.

Ellington was barely aware of Mackenzie screaming his name from somewhere else in the shed as Givens brought the fraction of board down again and again.

# CHAPTER THIRTY TWO

*"Jared!"*

Ellington's first name coming out of her mouth sounded odd, but it was the first noise her heart and lungs produced when the second attack from the two-by-four obliterated his left hand. Mackenzie banged helplessly on the container, watching it all play out. She knew Ellington was tough but there was a crazed sort of urgency to Givens's attacks that she had experienced firsthand.

She did notice that Givens wasn't able to get a full grasp on the two-by-four due to his own broken thumb—the thumb she had broken in a last-ditch effort before she'd been shoved into her cage. Hopefully that would take some of the power out of his swing.

She was about to yell again, hoping to maybe distract Givens, when a face suddenly appeared in front of the rectangular slats of the container. It was Missy Hale. Mackenzie had been so worried about Ellington that she'd nearly forgotten that Missy had been freed.

Missy looked back, making sure Givens was occupied, and then grabbed the bar holding the pin lock in. She had to put a bit of force into it but the bar clanged open. With another pull, the door opened up. Mackenzie started forward but then saw that Givens was advancing toward them, the splintered two-by-four drawn over his head.

Mackenzie shoved Missy out of the way just as the board came sailing down. It struck the side of the container, splintering the remainder of the board in half. Mackenzie used the jolt of the impact to her advantage and delivered a sweeping kick to Givens's shins. She put as much force as she could into it and he nearly lost his feet. But her back was still in excruciating pain and she was not able to put all of her strength into it.

Crying out in pain, she delivered a right-handed jab as he staggered against the container. It caught him in the chin and when his head rocked back, she delivered an open-handed palm strike to his throat.

He gagged and looked at her with wide, shocked eyes. She had busted his lip and his brow was still bleeding; the entire left side of his face was a sheet of blood. She tried to draw back for another punch but her back locked up on her. The bad news was that she was immobilized in that moment but the good news was that it made her certain that whatever was going on back there was only muscular, not spinal.

As he came at her, Ellington cut him off in a football-style tackle. Both men went to the floor in front of the container. Ellington had the upper hand but she saw that he was unable to use his left hand as a result of the board attack. As she watched, Givens brought a hard right hand up, catching Ellington in the side of the face. The bastard had been shot three, maybe four times and was still finding the strength to fight.

Mackenzie ran over to help but as Ellington fell off of Givens and the psycho got to his feet, he sprang at her. He was going for her knees in a football tackle–style attack. The shots he had taken had slowed him, though. Mackenzie was easily able to sidestep him. When she did, he slammed directly into the side of the container that had been holding Missy. The impact broke the chicken wire sheet from the front lip of the crate and the chicken wire fell over him. He fought with it, trying to get to his feet.

Mackenzie wasn't having it, though. She drew the gate of the container open as far as it would go and then slammed it, catching him in it. He howled and kicked out for her, striking her bad knee. She felt herself falling, unable to stop, and collided with him on the floor in a tangle of arms and legs. As they fought for position, her fingers found the chicken wire. They were both tangled in it, but she had more leverage and better position.

She bunched the wire into her fists. She could feel it cutting into her palms but she did not care. She clenched it tight and pushed down against his neck.

His eyes grew wide as she placed all of her strength into it. Every movement was beyond painful, jolts of sharp pain racing down her back and into her legs. She pushed past it, knowing that she *had* to. Beneath her, he started to choke.

*You have to stop,* she thought. *Let him live. Get some answers.*

But she remembered what it was like to be in that cage. She thought of the other women he had taken and placed in those same cages. She thought of him tracking them down on the back roads…and she was unable to stop.

*"Mackenzie, stop!"*

It was Ellington. His hands were on her arms and he was lifting her off of him.

He drew her off of Givens and she wanted to cry. She wasn't sure why but she could feel it boiling up inside of her. Ellington started to lower himself down to Givens but didn't bother. Whether it was the gunshots or Mackenzie's final assault, he wasn't moving. He was still alive, his breaths coming in hard and laborious pushes, but he wouldn't be getting up anytime soon. Mackenzie noticed

168

Missy Hale at the front of the barn, looking at him like a child might observe a coiled snake.

"You okay?" Mackenzie asked her, distracting herself from the weeping fit that was still trying to break through.

Missy only nodded.

"How about you?" she asked Ellington.

"A few fingers busted up, but I'll be okay. You?"

"I'm fine," she said through clenched teeth. The need to cry was passing but the pain in her back was terrible. Prideful or not, she was not going to show a sign of weakness until Givens was in the back of a patrol car. "Call this in, would you? He sort of destroyed my phone."

Ellington reached for his phone to do just that when a strangled voice stopped him.

"Sorry…"

It was Givens, speaking through blood and a choked wind supply. Mackenzie and Ellington looked down at him, weary and a little disgusted.

"Well then, I'm going to have Missy make the call. You good with that?"

"I just wanted someone to love me," Givens said.

Mackenzie recalled his obscure references to love while sitting in his living room and a chill rode down her spine. There was genuine pain in his voice, a clear confusion that reminded Mackenzie that even the most sadistic of people had a broken part of them that was vulnerable and human down at the core of it all.

It was a thought that stuck with her, clinging to her thoughts like cobwebs, until the night was broken by the sound of police sirens five minutes later.

169

## CHAPTER THIRTY THREE

As the night stretched on toward midnight, two things became clear: first, both Mackenzie and Ellington were going to the hospital; second, Harry Givens was not going to live to see morning.

Mackenzie's back had started to spasm and the right side of her face had swollen more than she'd thought from the hammer blow she had taken there. As for Ellington, two fingers on his left hand were broken. From the looks of it, Mackenzie thought the damage extended down into his hand. Through all of it, though, the thing that hurt Mackenzie worst of all was that with Givens likely dying, he would not be able to give the location of the missing women. Although Delores had said she heard another woman's voice in the other shed, that shed turned out to be empty.

Mackenzie and Ellington were both sitting in the back of Bateman's patrol car as Officer Roberts, in the passenger seat, made the call to hospital in Cedar Rapids, letting them know that two FBI agents would be headed their way soon. Bateman was driving, but had very little to say.

The little he did have to say had come in the form of a phone call several minutes ago. It had come from Wickline at the station, giving the little bit of information the paramedics and Givens's brief criminal record had to offer.

"Givens says there were five women in all," Bateman said. "He took the first almost a year ago, so he apparently had nothing to do with Vicki McCauley. That's all he was able to tell the paramedics before he passed out. We don't know where he took them or if they are even alive. As you know, the other shed turned up empty. But indications are that he got rid of whoever was in the container pretty recently."

"Any word on where Crystal Hall and Naomi Nyles are?" Ellington asked.

"No. They say he only spoke for about ten seconds. He's in pretty bad shape."

Mackenzie thought she heard blame in his voice. That was okay, though. As an officer, he understood that they did what was necessary in order to survive. Still, she could also tell that Bateman was more than ready to be rid of them.

Mackenzie recalled Givens saying *"I just wanted someone to love me..."* and for some reason, she felt certain that the women he had taken were alive.

"When we're cleared at the hospital, we can help with the search if you like," Mackenzie said.

"You're welcome to," Bateman said. "But we've got five teams of men out looking for Crystal Hall and Naomi Nyles. When the snow melts in a few days, it'll be easier, but by then…"

"Sounds good," Mackenzie said, knowing where he was going by trailing off.

"By the way," Bateman said, "you might find interesting what Wickline and some of the others at the station were able to pull up on Givens. Seems he spent most of his childhood seeing a psychiatrist. His mom got routinely abused in front of him by a father that later went on to kill himself. And then in college, he was involved in an almost-kidnapping where he snapped on an ex-girlfriend by not letting her out of the car while driving across three states."

*Sort of perfect in terms of painting a picture of what I'd expect a guy like Givens to be like,* she thought. *How did he go so long without snapping like this? And how did he stay under the radar for so long?*

They were both scary thoughts.

"You didn't have to drive us to the hospital," Mackenzie said, trying to eliminate the tension within the car.

"Please," Ellington said beside her. "You can barely walk. And you can't drive that well when you're *not* all busted up."

Bateman and Roberts chuckled in the front and for a moment, things seemed okay. This was especially true when Ellington reached over with his good hand and took hers. She nearly pulled it away out of instinct but, instead, gave his a squeeze.

"You were awesome tonight," he whispered. "I got to see that stubborn streak of yours that usually pans out for the good. I think the bureau needs to start paying attention to that."

"I wasn't *so* awesome. I did end up in a cattle cage."

"True. But you found the guy and led me right to him. And I was there earlier in the day. I could have prevented that happening to you and I didn't. And if it weren't for you, I'd be dead in that same barn right now."

She wasn't sure what to say to that. The way he was looking at her, speaking to her, and holding her hand…it was new to her. She could not remember the last time someone had cared so much about her. Sure, Bryers had done so there near the end, but with the chemistry between her and Ellington, it was different.

It was exciting and filled her with a weird sort of hope that she did not fully understand. And *that* was why it was so scary.

She gave him a smile and released his hand.

Outside, the snow blazed by in white streaks. Somewhere out there in that world of white, two women were missing—alive or dead was anyone's guess. She'd been unable to find them and while she knew she was not responsible for them, she did feel as if she had failed them. She thought of Bryers and wondered what sort of pep talk he'd give her.

Of course, her old partner was gone, no longer part of that world of white. And while she technically had a replacement partner in DC, the feeling of Ellington beside her made her feel safe. More than that, it made her feel *connected* to something. And she had not felt that in a very long time.

They rode on in silence, finding comfort in the discomfort of the other. It was a world filled with darkness.

And she felt a deep conviction rising once again in her veins: she wouldn't stop until she had extinguished all of it.

# COMING SOON!


## BEFORE HE NEEDS
### (A Mackenzie White Mystery—Book 5)


From Blake Pierce, bestselling author of ONCE GONE (a #1 bestseller with over 900 five star reviews), comes book #5 in the heart-pounding Mackenzie White mystery series.

In BEFORE HE NEEDS (A Mackenzie White Mystery—Book 5), FBI special agent Mackenzie White finds herself summoned to crack a case she has never encountered before: the victim is not a man or a woman—but a couple.

The third couple found dead in their homes this month.

As Mackenzie and the FBI scramble to figure out who would want happily-married couples dead, her search takes her deep into a disturbing world and subculture. She quickly learns that all is not what it seems behind the picket fences of perfectly-suburban homes—and that darkness lurks at the edge of even the happiest-seeming families.

As her hunt morphs into a deadly game of cat-and-mouse, Mackenzie, still struggling to find her own father's killer, realizes she may be in too deep—and that the killer she seeks may be the most elusive of all: shockingly normal.

A dark psychological thriller with heart-pounding suspense, BEFORE HE NEEDS is book #5 in a riveting new series—with a beloved new character—that will leave you turning pages late into the night.

Book #6 in the Mackenzie White Mystery series will be available soon.

Also available by Blake Pierce is ONCE GONE (A Riley Paige mystery—Book #1), a #1 bestseller with over 900 five star reviews—and a free download!

## Blake Pierce

Blake Pierce is author of the bestselling RILEY PAGE mystery series, which includes seven books (and counting). Blake Pierce is also the author of the MACKENZIE WHITE mystery series, comprising five books (and counting); of the AVERY BLACK mystery series, comprising four books (and counting); and of the new KERI LOCKE mystery series.

An avid reader and lifelong fan of the mystery and thriller genres, Blake loves to hear from you, so please feel free to visit www.blakepierceauthor.com to learn more and stay in touch.

## BOOKS BY BLAKE PIERCE

### RILEY PAIGE MYSTERY SERIES
ONCE GONE (Book #1)
ONCE TAKEN (Book #2)
ONCE CRAVED (Book #3)
ONCE LURED (Book #4)
ONCE HUNTED (Book #5)
ONCE PINED (Book #6)
ONCE FORSAKEN (Book #7)

### MACKENZIE WHITE MYSTERY SERIES
BEFORE HE KILLS (Book #1)
BEFORE HE SEES (Book #2)
BEFORE HE COVETS (Book #3)
BEFORE HE TAKES (Book #4)
BEFORE HE NEEDS (Book #5)

### AVERY BLACK MYSTERY SERIES
CAUSE TO KILL (Book #1)
CAUSE TO RUN (Book #2)
CAUSE TO HIDE (Book #3)
CAUSE TO FEAR (Book #4)

### KERI LOCKE MYSTERY SERIES
A TRACE OF DEATH (Book #1)
A TRACE OF MUDER (Book #2)

Made in the USA
San Bernardino, CA
09 May 2020